YOU GOTTA KNOW THE TERRITORY

Betrayal, Revenge, and Retaliation

—A MURDER MYSTERY—

JEROME RABOW, PH.D.

ISBN 978-1-953223-06-7 (paperback)

Rushmore Press LLC
1 800 460 9188
www.rushmorepress.com

Printed in the United States of America

CHAPTER 1

As he was getting ready to depart for work, Detective Joe Zuma kissed his wife of three years on the cheek, once again, admiring her peacefulness and beauty as she lay sleeping. He felt lucky and blessed to have Claudia who brought passion with her love for him and whose work as a painter of landscapes contrasted so sharply to his daily life of dealing with murderers. The last thing he looked at before he left to work every morning was the landscape of the beach and bay in Truro, Massachusetts, where they had first met.

It would usually take ten minutes to traverse the two miles from the northern part of the small town of Santa Monica where Zuma lived to get to downtown Santa Monica and arrive at his precinct. It was always an enjoyable ride as he never tired and always admired the blue Pacific, which could be seen as he traveled down Ocean Avenue. This morning, as he approached his office, the traffic became impossible. He was surprised to see so many news people and spectators in front. He knew immediately that something had happened to someone famous who lived in Santa Monica. Santa Monica had become the city where actors, directors, agents, and sports stars had bought homes. Unlike East LA and the rest of the greater Los Angeles area, it had air that you could breathe 360 days a year without alerts from the health authorities to stay indoors and avoid exercise. With the best air in the Los Angeles area, cool evening breezes, high-end and varied restaurants, a place for walking or jogging with views of the ocean, and excellent private schools, it was a city that only the affluent could now afford. All homes were sold in a day or so, usually with a bidding war that made real estate agents happy and frustrated the bidders. The less affluent that still lived in the city were able to do so because of the cities policy of rent control. The mixture of rich and poor, all white, was one of thing Zuma liked about the city. Less likeable was the fact that the only people of color seen in the city were the gardeners and housekeepers who had travelled in from East LA or those housekeepers who lived in the homes of their employers and who walked their children in the morning. The joggers who passed them rarely look at their faces but more often they would admire and smile at the faces of the white children in their $1,000 strollers. On those mornings when Zuma happened to be near some of the Santa Monica bus stops and seen the passengers getting off, he could imagine the bus that having come straight from Mexico instead of East LA.

He called to his assistant and told him to open the rear door so he could avoid the TV cameras and crowd. He cursed at himself for not listening to the news on the way in to work so he would know what was going on. Pat, the detective who worked closely with him, greeted him with a good morning.

"Okay, Pat, what do we know?"

"Boss, I got the call at about six thirty this morning from a woman who identified herself as the girlfriend of Richie Slater. She went out of her way to indicate that he was a famous and very successful Hollywood director She said she was sitting upstairs as she spoke with me and there were two bodies downstairs in the living room. I told her not to touch anything and that I would be arriving in ten minutes with two other officers. I told her she had to go downstairs and make sure the front door and all other doors were locked."

"And what did you find when you got there?"

"The front door lock was not jimmied with and the girlfriend who opened the door was pretty shaken up. I asked her to stay with one of the men while we went thought he rest of the house to see if anyone might still be there. When we went downstairs, I asked her to lead us to the living room where she had found the bodies. The room was neat, nothing broken or on the floor. The windows were locked.

The two bodies were lying on their backs. There was a lot of blood. Each one had been shot twice.

"Was the second body a male or female?"

"Female, with ID name Alice Bourne. I put a call in to have someone go to her residence to see if anyone else lived there."

"And you did all of this, this morning before I arrived at the office?"

"Yeah, boss, I wanted you to get a good night's rest. Aside from the guy being famous, it was pretty routine once we got to the scene."

"Thanks, Pat, I appreciate getting the extra winks, and it sounds like you did exactly what I would have done. If no one is home at the second vic's house, let's put an officer there to see who else might be living there If no one shows in forty-eight hours, we'll have to get a court order to enter and search her place. Let's head over to the home of the rich and famous director."

"We have the press outside. Do you want me or you speak with them?"

"No, let's go out the back way, and I'm sure they're already at the house. Let's deal with them there. I'll give them some of the details that you told me before we go into the house. That way we can get them to leave and make less commotion for the girlfriend."

"All right, gentlemen, all I can report now is it seems that two bullets were fired into Mr. Slater's heart. At this point, it does not appear to be a suicide. There is another victim inside. We now consider this a crime scene and we're going to do everything we can to solve this."

"Is the other body male or female? Can you give us a name?"

"It is a female, but I can give you no further information until we consult with the family. I have no further comments at this time, but I will keep you in touch with all developments in this case as they unfold. Now, if you'll please excuse me, I need to get back to work."

CHAPTER 2

Zuma and Pat saw the powder burns close to the two spots where the bullets had entered Slater's heart and noticed the angle at which they exited the body. He was wearing a speckled blue cravat around his neck which was now black in the places where the blood had reached. A gun was lying next to the body on the floor.

"Pat, he could have shot himself but that would be an unusual way of committing suicide. He would have had to pull the trigger with his thumb, and it would be hard to get off two rounds. It seems that someone was close enough to put the gun right up against his heart. The other vic was shot in the back. So, it's either one shooter hitting the two of them or two shooters, one killing Slater and another killing the woman."

"I agree, boss. I'll have the gun checked for prints and will do the whole house for fingerprints and footprints outside. There is no evidence of a forced entry. Are you ready to speak with the girlfriend? She's in the next room. She's pretty shook up. Pretty young. Name is Christina Marshall."

Chrisina Marshall walkied into the room with a confident walk. She was wearing a yellow robe and pink slippers. Her hair had a bit more orange color than the robe but they were very close in color. She appeared to be confident and in control.

"Ms. Marshall, can you tell us what happened? This might be a bad time for you, but since the details are fresh it would be helpful to us if you could go over what you remember. Take your time, any detail might prove to be important. If you feel you can't talk now or don't want to talk here, we can take you down to the station."

"I can do it now, Detective. I just need some water, and can you get those cameras off the lawn."

"No problem, Ms. Marshall."

"I was sleeping and hadn't realized that Richie had left and gone downstairs. I heard these two shots and I woke up. I realized he wasn't in the bed. I called out and didn't hear anything, so I hurried downstairs. I saw his body and another one next to his on the floor. His had blood all over his chest. I leaned down and tried to get him to talk. He didn't respond and I called 911."

"How did you know those were gunshots?"

"I didn't know. I only said that because I couldn't imagine what else they were."

"Did you feel for a pulse? Did you think he might be alive?"

"I was up so upset I never thought of that."

"Did you feel for a pulse on the other body?"

"That never occurred to me. As I just said, Detective, I was very upset."

"Did you recognize the other body?"

"No, I panicked, and I wanted to call 911 as fast as I could. She was lying face down, so I never even saw her face."

"What did you do while you were waiting for the police?"

"When I heard the sirens, I realized I only had my underwear on and it had his blood all over it, so I ran upstairs, changed and put on this robe."

"Please don't touch your underwear. We will pick it up. Can you tell us more about your relationship with Mr. Slater? How long have you known him? What were the living arrangements? This has nothing directly to do with the murder, but it might still lead us to the perpetrators."

"I met Richie when I was nineteen and a backup for a TV show. It was pretty quick for me. I had never been with an older man, and I was awestruck with his fame. I was suprised when he asked me to move in. I couldn't resist the idea of being with this famous man who wanted me to be with him and was interestd in my career. I moved in with him after three months."

"Do you know of anyone who wanted Mr. Slater killed?"

"Richie always said that there were a lot of directors who were upset with him because he wasn't going to help them or wouldn't want to collaborate with them. But I don't know any of them."

"And can you tell us about your relationship with Mr. Slater?"

"He wanted me to stop pursuing my career and told me I would not have to work because he would take care of me. I liked that idea. I wouldn't say I was a housewife type, but I was at his side whenever he wanted or needed me."

"And I hope you don't feel this is too personal, but can you tell us more about your financial arrangement?"

"He paid all the bills. I received three thousand a month. He was always generous to me. I'm not sure this has anything to do with his murder."

"Ms. Marshall, these are routine questions we ask of everyone close to the victim. I just have a few more. Did the two of you every fight?"

"No. He was annoyed that I hung around with my old fellow actors. He said they were losers and going nowhere. I didn't care if they were losers or not. They were my friends."

"Were any of them aspiring screen writers or directors?"

"Not that I know of. Some of them talked about it, but I never heard that any of them had actual experiences with directing or writing."

"Did any of them want to speak with your boyfriend?"

"Yes, Alice Bourne, but Richie did not want to speak with her. He said she was the leader of the loser crowd."

"Did he ever hit you?"

"Absolutely not. I had heard enough of that stuff when I was in the business to know that would be a red flag and a time to leave."

"We're almost done here, Ms. Marshall. Can you tell me if you have any family and did Mr. Slater have parents or children?"

"My parents live in LA. I have two brothers, but they still live in the South, and I'm not sure where. I know they left West Virginia. Richie had two boys and a daughter. He was somewhat estranged from all of them. I think when I moved in, it became more difficult for them to visit as we were all about the same age. His parents are deceased."

"Thank you, Ms. Marshall. If you can write down the names, phone numbers, and addresses of his children and that of your parents and any of the women you hung around with that would be appreciated. I also need to know the name and phone number of the accountant or the person who handled Mr. Slater's financial details. We may have to speak with you in the future as we uncover more aspects of the case.

After leaving the apartment and the car on the way back to the precinct, Zuma turned to Pat.

"What do you think, Pat?"

"She's a smart cookie for someone so young and she's pretty strong to be able to continue seeing her girlfriends after Mr. Success called them losers. It did seem a bit strange that as the interview went on, she was not at all stressed about the murder. She seemed eager to talk."

"I saw that also. Maybe she thinks this could be her opportunity. I'm sure she knows this will be primetime news for a few days and that reporters will be knocking on her door. She understands how the biz works and how this could potentially be a TV drama or a movie that could help her to go back and jumpstart her career a few rungs up from where she left off."

"We have a lot of names we're going to have to speak with, boss. Do you want to divide them up?"

"No, I'd rather work slowly and with you. Let's first do the home as you said before and wait for the medical examiners' report. Get her underwear, we might be able to pick up power burns if she did use the weapon from such close range. We need to check with Slater's accountant to see if there is life insurance and who the beneficiaries are. I think after that, we can start with Ms. Ingénue's parents."

"I'll put the names of all the people we need to interview on our board, boss. I'll call the accountant before the end of the day and tell him we are getting a court order so he can release all the financial records."

"Thanks, Pat. Can you ask him if he's willing to tell you the names of the beneficiaries?"

"Sure, boss. I'll make sure you know before you leave today."

Zuma called Claudia before he was about to leave the office.

"No, I knew you would not want to go out. Your face has been all over the news along with the grieving girlfriend. I picked up some food so no one would bother you if we dined out."

"After three years, you still are the perfect wife."

"I try to keep up with my perfect husband."

"Boss, there is only one beneficiary and it's the girlfriend. It's a whopping five million dollars. With that amount of cash, she is going to be able to dry and wipe away a lot of tears."

"We were right, Pat. She may have been young, but she knew how to look out for herself. The question for us is did she want that amount of cash as a long-term goal or was she counting on it in the short term."

"Well, boss, her short-term reality is that she can now hire the screenwriter to write her story, cast herself in the TV drama, and still have lots of bucks. And it looks like the long-term reality will be comfy also."

'I'm sure her loser friends will be looking for work and there will probably be a flock of others that Slater turned down or pissed off who may come a-knocking."

"As you always say, boss, this is Hollywood, and when there is big money involved, they come out of the woodwork. In this case, we are going to have a big cast."

"You're right, Pat, and I'm sure she'll be singing the words to a song that goes, *"Who's that knocking at my door, have I heard that knock before? Who's that tapping at my window? Who's calling me to go?"*

"Don't know that one, boss. Are there any songs you don't know the words to?"

Zuma laughed. "It's a take-off from an old nursey school rhyme, and I'm sure she'll be repeating it as they come calling."

CHAPTER 3

When Zuma arrived home, he was glad to see the table was set and ready for him and Claudia to dine.

"Would you like to talk and have a drink or eat first and then talk after dinner?"

"Let's eat first, honey. We can watch the different spins the TV newscasters are putting on Slater's death and I will let you in on the inside scoop of what we know or really of how little we know."

They sat quietly while enjoying the food that Claudia had picked up at Shangri-La, a hotel in Santa Monica. He loved their baked tuna, done similarly to the way the had often prepared it for Claudia when they were at Cape Cod.

They were a fulfilled and intimate couple, each secure in their own work. Zuma had received national attention from a drug bust in Orange County that netted over two dozen users and a couple of major dealers and had solved a case where one person had killed five adults, three of them men (including his own father) and two of them women. He also broke a drug-selling scheme in an elite private school in the community. As a result of all this attention he had been offered a position to head the Boston Police Department. It was a big honor and a huge pay raise, but in thinking about how much less time he would have with Claudia, he had decided not to accept the position. He knew he would be on call whenever Logan Airport was threatened, and the memory of the marathon bomber was still in all Bostonians awareness. They were extra sensitive, on the lookout for suspects and calling in lots of possible tips. His being nearer the cape was an upside, but knowing that he would be on call even if he was there made the job less appealing than it might have been a few years ago before Claudia. His boys would be proud but that was not that important to him. His policing methods that he trained his staff in stressed the use of nonviolence and talk with the last resort being force. The Department of Justice had assigned three people to study how Zuma trained his officers to be respectful towards all citizens and visitors to Santa Monica.

Claudia had an ongoing teaching position that allowed her, if she chose, to paint every day of the week. She loved working with the children, and the California sunlight had given her a new perspective on her outdoor landscapes. She now had a fairly large following of people who continued to buy her works. She was secure in her husband's love and devotion and his respect for her and her work.

Zuma turned the TV on and began switching channels and listening to the newscasters talk below headlines on the lower part of the TV tube.

Did Slater Slay Self?
Young Starlet finds Older Lover Dead.
Successful Director Found Dead by Less Successful Girlfriend.
Slain Screenwriter Slater.

"I think People magazine has inspired all this kind of slick headlining and garbage reporting."

The pictures and interviews with Ms. Christina Marshall stressed the grief she was experiencing except for one commentator who said she would be crying all the way to the bank. Zuma jumped up.

"How did they find out who the beneficiary of the insurance was? And besides the guy had two kids so I'm sure there will be legal challenges."

"Joe, calm down, tell me, if you want, what you know."

"The girlfriend was sleeping upstairs when she was awakened by what she thought were gunshots. When she went downstairs to look for the boyfriend, she found him dead, lying on the floor with two bullets in his heart. There was another body that had also been shot, a female. She called 911 and that's all we know. Slater had three estranged children. He didn't like his girlfriend's friends. He referred to them as losers. Slater was not known as a gracious person in the biz. So, it looks like there will be a lot of work with a lot of possible suspects."

"Who are the suspects?"

"Everyone I mentioned. His kids, her loser friends, jealous and unsuccessful aspiring directors and writers."

"Okay, honey, sounds like it's going to be a busy day for you tomorrow. Let's go to bed."

Zuma welcomed the invitation. His sleeping with Claudia usually led him to feel energized in the morning. It was very different from the time that Zuma had lost his first wife.

A hit-and-run driver had killed Carole, his first wife. Zuma was unable to accept that the police were never able to find the driver. Paralyzed by this state of affairs, he started to track down all drivers in Los Angeles who had received a DUI over the past three years and made them account for their whereabouts on the night she was killed. It was also during this time that his heavy drinking began. After a number of drivers complained to the precinct that Zuma had harassed them about their driving record, he was asked to take a leave of absence or go on sick leave for three months. He realized that his career was in jeopardy and decided to begin going to AA meetings. The meetings helped him be aware that a lot of hit-and-run drivers would not have a record. He was shocked to realize how naive he had been. He had gone to meetings for ten years and now he no longer attended. He felt in control of his drinking.

It was about two years after that when he was vacationing in Truro, Massachusetts, that he met Claudia. It took him another year when he went back to Cape Cod that they became involved. It was an instantaneous, smoldering connection. It was not so much one of passion as it was the amalgamating of two metals to make something more brilliant. She was a landscape painter and her vistas of Cape Cod were many of the same ones he had loved to visit on bike or car before he met her. He loved space and he loved quiet. Her paintings of the landscapes at the cape readily spoke to those exact preferences of his.

Their three years together in Santa Monica had increased their closeness so they were now like a cashmere glove that fit perfectly and smoothly. Sometimes she was inside and sometimes he was. She knew from the songs he was humming what was going on his mind and he knew from her voice that she was needing; time either for her work or her students. As they crawled into bed, she heard him humming Dylan's, "Blowin in the Wind." Claudia knew this meant that he was going to think and dream about all the suspects.

Pat Vasquez and Joe Zuma were also like a married couple each being to read the other and often anticipating what the other would say or do. Pat had the back door ready before Zuma arrived and Zuma had no need to call ahead. The press was out front again.

"Good Morning, Pat. Did you pick up anything since last night or shall we start from scratch?"

"I think it's starting from zero. Boss, I don't know how they found out who the beneficiary of the insurance was."

"The reporters won't say, so let's drop it. Were there any prints that showed up on the murder weapon that didn't match Slater's or the girls?"

"No, boss. The gun was clean Nothing back yet from our labs on the underwear. There was no forced entry and no footprints outside that were unique or different. The girl, Alice Munroe had published a short story and was an assistant director on a small independent movie."

"Pat, it looks like we have five people to get to. We can start with her parents and his three kids. That he's connected to the biz is going to make it more difficult for us to find time with the suspects. I'm sure they are all being interviewed and being promised big monies for their stories. Let's start with her parents. Get someone to go to the Munroe apartment and keep an eye on it to see who comes around. If no one shows up in the next forty-eight hours, we will need to get a court order so we can go in and look for anything that could be important to our case."

On the drive to Inglewood, Zuma smiled when he heard Pat humming the tune to Dylan's "Mr. Tambourine Man." Zuma had this habit of pulling a toothpick out of his left shirt pocket and humming "Blowin in the Wind." When Pat asked what the song was, Zuma told him to look up other Dylan songs to figure out which one it was. Pat made a few wrong guesses before he guessed the correct tune, but in the process of looking up Dylan songs, he had grown to love many of them, especially "Mr. Tambourine Man." Pat felt that he, Pat, would always be willing to "come following Zuma," his boss.

The drive to Inglewood was a short one, and the two detectives pulled up in front of an older, small two-bedroom apartment. After identifying themselves, Mr. Marshall unlatched the chain and let them in. The stench hit them immediately. It was a combination of cat litter, dirty dishes, and dust.

"Mr. and Mrs. Marshall, this is part of the routine calls we must make with people who know your daughter and her husband. Thank you for letting us in and we hope you can talk freely with us."

She replied, "We can tell you all whatever you'all like to know. We have nothing to hide from y'all."

Zuma and Pat recognized a southern accent though they knew it was not from the Deep South.

"Well, tell us what life was like for your daughter growing up in…?"

"West Virginia, Detective. We're mountain people. You may know our state is called the mountain state. We're from a small town that our great grandparents were also born in. Christina is a fourth generation of Marshalls to be born there. Everyone knew everyone in the town, and we were after four generations of living in one town, kin to one another. Christina was a beautiful girl and she always wanted to get to the movies. When she got this role in the high school musical of Oklahoma, the boys came sniffing around. She was sixteen, and we were afraid she would get knocked up and ruin her life, so we whisked her away to the big city. I left my work. I was a foreman for the coal company in our town. Left a good pension behind, but we wanted to look after Christina. We came to LA and tried to do everything we could to ensure she would hit it big. She didn't want to go to school and began showing up as an extra on the sets of different movies and TV shows. That's how she met her then-to-be husband."

"How did you afford her lessons?"

"Detective, we are mountain folk and if it's anything we do know about it's hard work. Like that song says, 'our souls are made out of muscle and bone.' We both got jobs during the day and I would work extra on weekends. We would take any kind of work. We are not proud or afraid of hard work."

"And what did you think of Mr. Slater? Did you ever get the chance to meet him before they got together?"

"We were worried that he was so much older, but we were hopeful that he could be helpful to her career. He looked down at us, thinking we were hillbillies or mountain folk. But we could over look that as long as Christina seemed happy."

"Did he ever use those terms, 'hillbillies' or 'mountain folk' to you directly?"

"No, Christina told us that's how he referred to us."

"Did you give any advice to her?"

"Yeah, we'all told her to make sure she would get something besides her monthly allowance and support for her career. We brought up the idea of an insurance policy. At first, she thought it was unnecessary, but she came around."

"How do you feel about his death?"

"To tell you the truth…we only think it can mean good things for our daughter."

"And for yourselves?'

"Yes, I suppose that too. She'll have money now for all the lessons she will need and have a little nest egg for her future."

"Did she give an allowance to you?"

"As a matter of fact, she did. She was generous and she gave us $1250.00 per month."

"Do you think Mr. Slater knew about this?"

"I don't know. I don't think so. She told us not to mention it to him. He'd probably think we would be wasting it."

"Did you need the money or were you able to put some away for savings?"

"Some months we saved and others we didn't. They keep raising the rent in this shithole, so it's hard for us to save and we just can afford another place and we don't want to move far away from Christina. She's not our only child, but she is the one who stays in contact with us."

"And your others?'

"They haven't spoken to us since we moved Christina to Hollywood. We're not even sure where they are living. It could be their home town in West Virginia or some other area of the South. We don't think they came north. They might be in touch with Christina, but she doesn't tell us about them. Once she made it clear that she would not be talking to us about them, we stopped asking questions."

"Why do you think they stopped talking to you?"

"They may have been angry that we choose Christina over them and that we left the place that our family had lived in for over four generations. In a way, I don't blame them. I feel that as men they would be less likely to feel trapped."

'One final question, please, do you know any of Christina's current friends?"

"Yes, her friend Alice left Tennessee the year after her and she and Christina mentioned that they were in contact and saw each other. They had been good friends in high school. I think Christina helped her when she came out here with some housing."

"Would that be Alice Bourne?"

"Yes, that is her name."

"Okay, Mr. and Mrs. Marshall, thank you for your help with this. One more question. Do either of you have a key to Christina's residence?"

"We do. Christina gave us one so we could go there and get away from this shithole. She and the boyfriend would go away three or four times a year for long four-day holidays. She just made us leave the place exactly as we found it. We were pretty careful about doing that, so I don't know he ever knew."

Zuma and Pat were glad to get out and breathe the fresh air.

"Well, Pat, what do you'll think about her parents?"

"I think Boss, the only things that are real and I can trust was their accent, their smells and the keys?"

Zuma laughed. "I think your right, Pat. We will keep them on our radar, and we know that mountain people learn at an early age on how to use guns. They hunt squirrels and possums for food. They must both be good shots and we can assume that Christina also knew how to use a weapon. Right now, we need to keep our surveillance on the apartment of the girlfriend, Alice Bourne. Pat, let's go meet the children of Mr. Slater."

CHAPTER 4

Two of Slater children, Sammy and Sarah Slater lived together in a small two-bedroom on the edge of Culver City and Playa del Rey. They were neither welcoming nor cold about the invitation to talk about their father. They just seemed indifferent.

"Can you tell us how you heard the news about your father's death?"

"On the TV. That slimy girlfriend didn't fool us. She ain't grieving. She was after our father's money."

"What makes you think that?"

"When Dad introduced us, she made no effort to be nice. We already had some problem with him, but she added to them. At least we were talking before. Yes, we argued about our careers and work, but he only yelled at us. He never stopped talking. When she came into the picture, the talking stopped."

"What did you specifically argue about?"

"Dad wanted us to get into the SAG union as set designers or costume designers. He felt that neither of us could make it as actors. We disagreed. We just get by now. I'm a cocktail waitress in an upscale Hollywood restaurant and Sam works as a maître'd in the same restaurant. Dad helped us get those jobs."

"Did you ever see your father and Christina fight? Did you ever see either of them hit each other?"

Sarah looked at Sam.

"I did see him smack her once on the side of her head. He then turned around and threw something at a window in the living room and broke the glass. He apologized right away when he saw the blood, but I could tell that this was probably not the first time because as he came near her, she pushed him away as if to say. 'You did it again.'"

"What did you hear her say to him that caused him to get so angry?"

"She was teasing him about his age and how cheap he was."

"Do either of you own a gun?"

"No, Detective."

"And do either of you have a key to your dads' home?"

"No, again."

"Do you know of anyone who would want to have your dad killed?"

"You mean aside from Christina?

"Yes."

"I know our dad was disliked by many in the business, but he was also respected. But I don't have any names for you or know anyone. Do you Sarah?"

"No."

"If any names pop up, could you give us a call? And if anything occurs to you about who might have been involved with this murder, please let us know. Can you give us the phone number of your brother please? I'd venture a guess that his name also begin with an S?"

"You got it, Detective. It's Saul."

"The case is growing, boss."

"Yes, it is, Pat. We've got two parents who would probably pimp out their daughter and who have a key so they could gain entrance, a not-too-grieving girlfriend, and three kids who are all estranged from their father. Plus, there are an unknown number of others who might be angry with Slater for his lack of cooperation or help. That's six definite names and we haven't even touched the network of Alice Bourne, the friend of Christina. But first, let's check on the other child of Mr. Slater."

Saul Slater ran a tattoo parlor on Hollywood Boulevard near Vine. He was the only one behind the counter and his arms were fully tatted. His very short, lightly colored blue shorts with red polka dots showed his tatted thighs and legs down to his red socks. Zuma saw the "only in Hollywood look" on Pat's face.

"Hi, Mr. Slater, we're here as part of our routine investigation to interview all close friends and relatives of the victim."

"I don't think I'm close exactly. I'm his son in name only."

"When was the last time you saw or spoke with your dad?"

"Probably a year ago. But before then it must have been over 5 years."

"What was the occasion?"

"He asked me to give a tat to his girlfriend."

"Did you?"

"Sure, Detective. He paid for it."

"What did it say and where is it?"

"That's confidential. You can check with her."

"Had you ever met her before or since?"

"No, Detective."

"Why were you estranged?"

"I didn't want to have anything to do with the biz. He thought I was good-looking enough, and with some acting classes I could make a go of it. I wanted nothing to do with it. This is honest work I do, and I make people happy. It doesn't depend on critics or advertising. I control the pace of it. My father had no respect for what I do."

"And why is it that you don't see your siblings very often?"

"No reason. We're not estranged or anything like that. We're all busy. They each have small tats near their ankles, which I did for them. We're friendly."

"Do you know of anyone who want to kill your Dad?"

"I don't know anyone, Detective, but I'm sure there must be quite a few. He was not liked."

"Are you aware that you will get some money from an insurance policy?"

"Really? No, I wasn't and frankly, I'm a little surprised. I thought the old codger had completely given up on me as his son. I'm sure he would find it pretty ironic that if I do get some money, I will be able to expand my business. I have wanted to do that for a while. Even I think this location is a bit too seedy for me and even for some of my clients. My old man would not be happy to see me expanding the business. He did not want me to be successful in a tattoo parlor business. Life sure has it's ironies, Detective."

"And its weird color," said Zuma to Pat as they exited the parlor.

CHAPTER 5

"Boss, the Chief of the LA Police Department is outside. Says he knows he didn't call ahead because he didn't want any attention. He says it's important and would like to speak with you now."

"Send him in, Pat, and don't leave. Even if wasn't important, I would let him in."

Chief Thompson was sixty-four years old, six feet two inches and about 35 pounds over his ideal weight of 175. He could have retired but did not feel there was much else he wanted to do. He took pride and often let it be known that he managed one of the largest police departments in the country. Zuma though he had a big ego.

"Thanks for seeing me, Detective. We have had minimal contact, but I know of your work and am here to ask you for your services. Do you want your aide to stay?"

"Yes, Detective Vasquez and I work very closely but even before you ask, and this may be presumptuous of me, but I am not ready to fill your shoes."

Thompson laughed heartily. "And I'm not ready to take them off yet. I have a more limited request. Let me state it. We have a precinct that does not do well with the citizens it is responsible for. There have been too many officer shootings at citizens and more lawsuits from the citizenry than many of my precincts combined. The city is on my back about the amount of money they have to spend on these lawsuits. I want you to come in and train my officers. You have an excellent reputation for instilling in the people who work for you a sense of respect and responsiveness to the citizens of your city, Santa Monica. I want you to come in and do the same with this one precinct that is out of control."

"I'd have to get the approval of my boss. Do you have any idea of how long this will take? He will want to know."

"I've already spoken to him and he is in agreement. If you do a good job, it will make this precinct and your precinct look better. I have agreed to provide some manpower to replace you. More boots on the ground to help with investigations."

"I'm interested. But I have two concerns. I have a case now that involves two murders and I would like to work closely with my aide, Pat Vasquez."

"You could bring Vasquez with you. I think his being Latino would help my officers to be a bit more receptive to your training."

"Pat, would you want to go with me and be willing to let our case be supervised from downtown LA?"

"Sure, boss. I would look forward to that. I think I may know a couple of the guys who work from that precinct. Maybe they could be the ones that are assigned to our current case."

"Okay, Chief Thompson. I will have to discuss this with my wife. I know this will make a big change in my schedule as there are bound to be more issues than the teaching of respect."

"Thank you, Detective Zuma, I would hope to get an answer from you after you are able to discuss this with your wife. Detective Vasquez, if your boss says yes, we can discuss who your pals are in the precinct and whether I can afford to let them go."

"Pat. What do you think?"

"Seems like a straightforward request."

"It's straightforward all right, but I wonder if he did this because of pressure from the justice department, not only from the lawsuits and charges of racism but for some other stuff."

"What kind of stuff?"

"I'm not sure, but sometimes, these things could be due to some internal practices and someone blows a whistle because they get pissed off. Just let's keep our eyes open."

"Claudia, we need to go out to dinner. Something big has come up. No, nothing to worry about. It's an opportunity for me but it could affect us."

"Sure, Joe, I'll make a reservation at the Shangri-La.

"Claudia, I got this visit from the Chief of the LA Police Department, and he wants me to train some of his men who are not behaving very responsibly towards the citizens in their precinct. It sounds straightforward, but I have the feeling that a lot more could be going on than just mistrust or fear of the citizens. So, it might mean longer days, and I want to know if you would be prepared for that. I'd like to do it. Pat will be working with me and that makes it even more appealing. The chief said he would provide some manpower to take over my cases while we supervise them. It feels like a clean offer and a neat package."

"Darling, this sounds like a wonderful opportunity and it gives you a chance to do what you love to do—to teach officers what it means to protect and serve. And I will be fine. I have my teaching and my painting, and whatever part of you I can, even if it is only minimal, I will treasure."

Zuma knew he could always count on Claudia to support what he wanted but the ways she did it and the words she spoke always shocked him. It was done with ease and grace and deep affection.

"I'm also thinking of opening my own gallery so that may take up a lot more of my time. I haven't done much planning, but I think I've located a place. I'll keep you posted as soon as I know more about it."

"Let's order, Claudia, and make a toast to our new ventures."

"I know, Joe, these new things in our lives will strengthen us even more although I can't imagine how that would be possible."

"Let me call Thompson now with my affirmative, so he has the message when he gets in tomorrow morning. I'm sure he would appreciate knowing when he starts his day."

"Boss, Thompson called and said we could start tomorrow. He's going to wait for us to talk about who he could send over to work on our case."

"Let's get the chart ready for the guys who are coming in. We want to be able to work closely with them. We should have some assignments ready for them. I think following up with interviews after they get to know the case would be the best thing we can do for the case and for easing them in."

That shouldn't take long, boss. How do you want to spend the rest of the day? Do we need to prepare for tomorrow?"

"No prep on my part or on yours. I'd like you to walk in not knowing what I have planned so your impressions can be to what they are doing and not to what you have thought about they might be saying. As for the rest of the day, this is what I had in mind. Let's' search the Munroe apartment and see what we can find in the way of correspondence and connections between her and Christina and, possibly, Slater."

The call came in on the drive over.

"Detective Zuma, this is Officer Hodge, I knew you would want to hear about this as soon as the call came in. Saul Slater was found in his car, just off the 101 Freeway near Studio City. It was close to his siblings' house. He had been shot and was dead when the report came in. I'm at the scene of the shooting right now."

"Thanks, Hodge, well head right over. Don't touch anything and put the yellow plastic up. We should be there in ten minutes."

"Boss, so now there are three vics but one less suspect. Too bad we have to do the training tomorrow."

"He is a vic but that doesn't mean he couldn't have done the other shootings. Let's see what we can discover to help the new boots."

Saul Slater had been shot in the head through the driver's window. Witnesses reported that he had stopped at a red light with another car next to his. When the light turned green, two shots were fired and the car took off. The people who had been witnessed the shooting were waiting off to the side, away from the vehicle with Saul's body, and an officer standing next to them.

"Thank you for waiting, ladies and gentlemen. Can any of you identify the car that took off or did any of you see a license plate?"

"We were at the curb and the light indicated about four second left so all of us decided not to cross. When the light turned green, we heard two shots and the car just sped away. It was a dark brown Ford, pretty old. I don't think any of us knew the year. That's what we already told your other officer."

"Well, thank you again for repeating this. We like to get your names, just in case you have to be called as witnesses later on. We appreciate your waiting. Would you say that the getaway car was drive by a male or female?"

"We couldn't come to any agreement about that. A few of us were convinced it was a male and a few thought it was a female. So, I guess the answer is no."

"Pat, this was not a random drive by. Whoever did this must have been tailing the victim."

"Why is that, boss?"

"They knew they would have to get away the moment the light turned green. My guess is the perp spent some time waiting for the time when their car could be next to the vic's and for them to be at the head of other lane."

"Boss, that could still is a random drive by."

"Yes, your right, Pat, but not if it's Saul Slater and the father, Richard Slater, is the other vic. That is too coincidental. Let's check his driving record for the past three weeks and can you grab his phone right now to see who he might have spoken to today and for the past three weeks? We need to check if he has had contact with anyone of the others connected to the case. While you're doing that, I'm going to alert Thompson of another victim that I believe is connected to this case."

"Boss, he had a call today and I recognized the number. This is going to be hard to understand or figure out."

"The only numbers you would recognize are my home, my cell, or the precinct. So, what is it?"

"You're right, boss, but it's one that was in our file on this case. It's the parents of Christiana, Mr. and Mrs. Marshall. Another number that seemed familiar, and I checked it, came in from the precinct that we are scheduled to do our training tomorrow."

"Pat, let's keep this to ourselves until we have a chance to figure out what might be going on and then we can speak to Chief Thompson. We can see who was at their desk at the time the phone call was made."

CHAPTER 6

"Hi everybody. My name is Joe Zuma and some of you may have had contact with me. I'm from the Santa Monica precinct and your chief has invited me in to address some problems that are occurring in your precinct. In the precinct that I come from, we pride ourselves in doing good police work. We do this without hitting or threatening or beating up our suspects. Brandishing our weapons is not something we do unless we have been notified that a suspect is dangerous or armed. So, if you come here believing or thinking you can do things you have seen police officers doing on TV or in the Harry Bosch novels, you're going to have to give those ideas up. We are here to vanquish you of those ideas and to more directly address your beliefs and practices. Detective Vasquez and I will train you to rely on our brains and our experiences. Bringing in a suspect who is going to sue the city or you personally is not what I or anyone else in this precinct wants to see.

You are being paid to do police work. That is all you are allowed to do. You cannot do your laundry, run errands for your family, or eat donuts on the job. You are never to accept anything from a grateful client and certainly not from a suspect. Finally, and most importantly, all the citizens who live here, visit here, or play here, deserve our respect. Do not act on any of your preconceived notions about race, gender, dress, or cars. If during the course of our training any of you feel you need guidance in this area, please see my assistant Detective Pat Vasquez, or me. We will not hold this against you. In fact, you will look better in our eyes if you can seek this training on your own. Any questions?"

"How long will the training last?"

"That's an important question, but I want to hold off on it now. A lot depends on how we work together."

"Isn't this going to mostly presentations by the two of you? What do you mean by working together?"

"I mean, we will talk to each other about what we do present."

"When do we start?"

"Our training will start tomorrow. You need to know that whatever we discuss in here stays in here. I will not be reporting anything about any one officer to your chief. I will only tell him about what we are doing and not what any of you say to me or to each other or about your boss. Again, I repeat, please see Pat or me for any issues you have with our training. Pat and I are here to help, and you are here to serve. If there are no questions you're dismissed."

"Is this time in training considered work time? Are we getting paid?"

"Yes."

"Detective, this is a personal question, so I know you don't have to answer but where does the name Zuma come from? I know it could be an Aztec name. Is your family from South America? Please forgive me, I am curious."

"Nothing to forgive. My grandfather loved the Marines as did my father and the Marine hymn included the phrase 'From the Halls of Montezuma.' When my father landed in this country with his father, my grandfather decided to change their name. I think it may have been more Spanish although my mother was Italian with a Greek background."

"Thank you. Did you speak Spanish in your family growing up?"

"No, it's something I regret. My father and grandfather, like so many other immigrants wanted us to Americanize, which unfortunately for me, meant no other language was to be spoken in our home except English."

"Nice job, boss. You handled all those questions without being defensive."

"Chief Thompson, have you decided who the three people you are going to provide to my staff to work on this case?"

"Yes, I have. They are officers Belcher, Álvarez and Pointer."

"We may have a problem with Belcher. He was on the desk and is probably the one who called Saul Slater before he was shot."

"Let's call him in right now. Do you want to handle it Zuma or shall I?"

"Let me take this, chief."

"Detective Belcher, you were on the desk yesterday and a call was made to Saul Slater. Did you make that call?"

"Yes, I did."

"And would you be willing to tell us why you called him?"

"I've always gotten my tattoos from him and I was scheduling another. Why, is there a problem?"

"One problem that I mentioned in our orientation has to do with the fact that you were conducting personal business. This is against departmental policy and I am going to suggest to Chief Thompson that this violation be put in your file."

"It will not happen again."

"A second problem which may not have anything to do with you or the phone call is that he was shot point blank through his car window yesterday while waiting for a traffic light to change. In checking all phone calls on his phone, this station came up which is why we called you in."

"I can assure you, Detective Zuma, I had nothing to do with that shooting. I was, as I said, calling for an appointment to get another tattoo."

"Detective Belcher, do I detect a bit of a southern accent in your speech?"

"Why, yes, you do. Very few people pick that up."

"And would it be possible that you were born in West Virginia?"

"Again you're right, Detective Zuma. John Denver made our mountain state famous. He said it was like heaven in those blue ridge mountains. I left there when I was eleven and the kids at my school in LA made fun of the way I spoke, so I worked hard to get rid of the accent. You're one of the few who picked it up."

"Thank you, Detective Belcher. Chief, I have no further questions."

"Belcher get back to work."

Belcher left.

"Do you still want him assigned to your precinct Detective Zuma? I'll do whatever you think is best."

"Pat, what do you think?"

"Pete Belcher is one of the people I said I knew at this precinct. I don't know him very well. We trained at the academy together. He was serious about the training and I thought of him as a straight shooter. I think he could be of more help working on the case. He knows at least one member of the Slater family. He might know more. It's a greater risk if he's covering up anything but it also could open up more likely leads. He would be good to interview Slater's other kids since he knew their brother and his tats might give them a sense of safety so that they would be freer to talk."

"Chief Thompson, now you see why I like working with Pat. Go ahead with the original assignment you made of the three officers. This will also give Belcher a sense that we are not suspicious of him, which may work to our advantage. If you can get them to report to us this afternoon, they will be ready to start tomorrow and we also will be ready to start tomorrow. At some point, we may need to get Belchers' phone to see if has been calling any others connected to this case."

"I can ask him to do it now."

No, let's wait. I don't want him to believe that he is a possible suspect."

CHAPTER 7

"Pat, when we get near the site, I want you to drop me off about a block away. I don't want anyone to see that I am around. You will go in and tell them you received a phone call from me, saying I would not be there and that you were told to take over the training. They may have some questions about my absence or your being in charge. Indicate you don't know anything more than what you told them. After that, ask them to take out a pencil and paper and write, "I treat all the people I serve in the same manner." Tell them we do not want their names but only their honest answers. When they have finished, underneath that ask them to write "Agree or Disagree." After they write their answer, tell them to write the phrase, "Have you personally felt that you have been treated differently from other officers who are not of your own race? If yes, leave a few lines for them do complete this. Repeat that we do not want to know their names but will need this information to do further planning. That's all.

"At that point, I will come in and take over. I will ask them to pass their answers to the front and you will collect them and tally the responses while I'm talking. Okay, Pat?"

"Sure, boss. I got it but have no idea of what you're going to do."

"That's the way I want it, Pat."

Zuma walks in as the officers are writing. They look up and a few have looks of surprise

having believed that Detective Vasquez was in charge of the training.

"Okay, so we developed this experience to see if you would discover any expectations you might have of seeing a person in color in charge rather than me, a white male. What were some of the things you felt?"

"I was a bit more relieved. I thought he'd be easier on us than you would."

Everyone laughed.

"I was concerned that we might not get credit for the training."

"I was worried that we would have to do the training over again. Since you were not doing it."

"I notice that none of the officers in this room had concerns that Vasquez, a man of color, would be harder on the officers in this room who are white."

Silence.

"I was happy to see that a man of my ethnicity was in charge. I thought he would understand me."

"May I assume that since one or possible more were happy to see Vasquez in charge that some of you weren't?" Again, silence. "I will take that silence as a yes. Now, what is the point of our doing this? What does it mean that some of you have different reactions to a person who is white and a person who is not white?" Silence again. "We designed this training to show that we have different expectations about people of different racial backgrounds."

"I don't think I felt anything different when I saw Vasquez instead of you. I treat all people the same.?

I think most of us feel the way you do, Officer…? What is your name?"

"Tucker."

"Yes, Officer Tucker, most of us think we do, but those whom we meet may not feel the same way. They might see differences in your actions based on seeing you in different situations. Pat, how many people said they treat all people in the same manner?"

"Fourteen of the twenty agreed with the statement. Six disagreed."

For the people who answered "Agree" would you be willing to acknowledge that if your child was a male, you would be treating them differently than if your child was female?'

"Yes, I wrote agree and I could see that I would do that."

"Let's talk about how we might treat our male children differently than our female children."

"I'd give my son more responsibilities. More chores."

"I would let him drive at sixteen but would not let my daughter do that."

"I would let my son date earlier and stay out late without questioning him."

"So if we treat a person differently based on gender, is it possible we treat people differently based on race?"

"That's not the same thing. People are born with a particular gender."

"People are born into a racial category or at least are assigned one either prior to or at their birth."

"Okay, you're right about that. But that does not mean I would treat them differently."

"No, it doesn't, but think for a moment about the words that are most frequently assigned to men of color." Silence. "Okay, let me tell you what we discovered when we do this with other officers. Here are the words that occur: violent, lazy, thief, liar, parolee, and hostile. And if it is a woman of color: crazy, welfare queen, whore, and slut."

So, if these are the representations that are presented to us in the media, newspapers, and TV, do you believe that they do not have any effect on how you treat the people you come into contact with? And how is Vasquez represented in the media? Undocumented, gardener, cheater, player, illegal, and border crosser. Again, do you think we can escape these messages that we receive daily?

"We have no more time to discuss how we deal with these messages and how they might affect us. However, before we go, let's look at the answers you gave to the question "Have you personally felt that you have been treated differently from other officers who are not of your own race. Pat, what did you find?"

"All twenty-one said yes."

"Thank you for your honesty. You are all dismissed. I will consult with your chief about the day and time of our next training."

On the way back to their Santa Monica precinct, Zuma asked Pat about the training.

"I liked it a lot. I especially liked how you put those words out for Black and Latinos. I personally have heard them all. I have often wondered how it was possible that you were never influenced by them."

Zuma smiled. "I work hard to keep fighting that stuff, Pat. It's something I find myself having to do almost daily since there is some much crap and garbage coming at me."

"What are you planning to do with the fact that every one of them said they have been treated differently by those who are not of the same race?"

"That's the heart of the training, Pat. And as you have heard me say before, 'more to be revealed.'"

The call came in from Thompson before the two had arrived at their precinct.

"You stirred up a hornet's nest here, Zuma. Five of the folks came in to tell me they fell you were accusing them of being racists. I told them since I was not there, I could not agree or disagree but told them to bring it up with you."

"You did the right thing, Chief Thompson. And the reaction is one that I was hoping for and it is hardly unexpected. Can we talk about scheduling the second training as soon as possible, maybe even tomorrow?"

"Zuma, if that's what it takes, I will tell the men now to be there at eight sharp."

"Boss, that was pretty emotional for me. Feels like the Slater case is distant."

"I'm sure it is, Pat. If you want to take the rest of the afternoon off, you can. I'm going to meet the new recruits and go over the case with them."

"Thanks, boss. Would it be ok if I sit in the back while you go over the details?"

"Absolutely okay. Im going to start right in."

"We have given you each a folder with all the names and interviews in the case. A name of another vic that needs to be added is Saul Slater. He was the son of the director and was shot yesterday. The report should be coming in shortly. Each of you will be working with one of our detectives who are already familiar with the case. I'd like you to works in teams as Pat and I do. Wherever possible, let's be as diverse as we can. You can each select whom you want to interview. Please introduce yourself to our team members. If you think that something besides or in lieu of an interview is important, feel free to use that judgment. Let's meet back here tomorrow in the afternoon. Do you have any questions?"

"Who is going to follow up with the vic who was just shot?"

"I don't think that matters too much. Why don't you decide and figure that out? There's a phone we have, so a bunch of names needs to be checked and folks who may need to be interviewed. I would like Belcher to work with the girlfriend or the parents of the girlfriend. There's a southern background and connection to this whole case and his understanding of that culture could be helpful."

Thank you, Detective Zuma. I'll give it my best."

"That was good, boss. I like that you gave them leeway to do whatever they think is important. And Belcher seemed to enjoy the confidence you have in him."

"It's confidence, Pat, but it maybe the confidence that arises from his thinking he can be a better position to protect himself."

"I think we can each leave a bit early today. The training takes something out of me also, Pat."

"Thanks, boss. I welcome that."

"Claudia, I don't know if you're working or not. I'm heading home early, and if you not there I'll be taking a nap. Let's go out to dinner at seven. I need to get up extra early as we will be doing the second training tomorrow morning. When I wake up around 6:45 and you're not there, I'll just meet you at the Shangri-La."

CHAPTER 8

"Detective Zuma, I want to start the training today by asking you a qustion. Would you mind if I do that?"

"Not at all. Pat and I always welcome quesions."

"I think you are trying to change us. I think you want us to see ourselves as racists. If that is the goal of the training, I for one feel annoyed. Is that your goal?"

A few of the men turn around nodding their heads appreciative of the question.

"Thank you for your directness and honesty. First, I don't think I can change anyone. So that is not my goal. My goal is for you to take a look at yourselves and behavior and to see if you are satisfied with it. If you are, then you will do nothing to change. If you are not pleased or unhappy, then you might try and do something. I repeat, you might or will try and do something. It is only you who can do it. I can't force you. Neither can your boss. So, to repeat, my goal is for you to hear and learn about your behavior as it impacts others—those whom you serve and those you work with. If you seek to try and change your own behavior, Pat and I will work with you to do that. Any further questions before we get started with our second day?"

"So, we're not going to be asked to prove a change in attitudes or answer questions meant to show how we have or haven't changed?"

"Correct. Any changes are strictly up to you. They are your own business. Your chief and I are not going to test you or ask you to prove if or how you have changed." Zuma waits. "Okay, let's pick up where we left off. All of you agreed that you have been treated differently by a member of a group that is not your own. That is, you see people acting one way when they are with their own racial group and another way when they are with you. Pat, could you read some of the answers written down yesterday? Remember, these were anonymous. We recognize that you might know who gave a particular response, but please do not indicate that you know who wrote it. Go ahead, Pat."

"When I walk to the water cooler, people stop talking about what they were talking about and change the subject. It makes me feel they don't like me and don't trust me."

"People talk more loudly to me than they talk to others. It makes me feel they think I am deaf and also dumb."

"When I tell a joke, people often don't smile or laugh. They just look at me as if I am stupid."

"I think the white officers, me especially, in this department, are seen as racists by the people of color."

"Okay, Pat, let's stop with those four. Were they repeated more than once, Pat?"

"Yes. Those were all checked at least four times."

"Does anyone want to respond to these? You do not have to identify yourself as the author of the phrase."

"I don't have a problem saying I wrote down the one about jokes. I am considered as the family comedienne. I always have jokes at our big family dinners and people count on me to supply a new batch every big holiday. There is lots of laughter. I don't get why the joke is not funny to my fellow officers."

There are nods of agreement while the speaker is talking.

"Is anyone willing to respond to that comment? Someone, perhaps, who has not found some jokes to be at all humorous."

"I will respond. When you told the joke about the people on welfare, you were talking about my aunt and my sister and my brother-in-law. I did not think the joke where the punch line was 'If you can afford cigarettes, you don't need welfare' shows any sensitivity about what being without a job does to people. Cigarettes may be a way of dealing with their loss. You do not show any sensitivity to those lives."

"Well, maybe you're too sensitive."

"You know, you're right. I am too sensitive. But I'm not sensitive for reasons you probably believe. I wasn't born sensitive. I have been made sensitive. I'm sensitive to all those jokes about welfare queens and people who have children so they can collect more welfare. And all those jokes are about my people. You know goddamn well they are not about white people. So, when I hear you start a joke about welfare, I shut down. I frown. 'Here it comes,' I say to myself. Another white dude stereotyping and being grossly insensitive."

"Let's stop the discussion about this now. We will come back later to it, but I'd like to get at least one more comment. Can we go to the water cooler comment? Anyone?"

A white police officer stood up. "I can. I always get the cold shoulder when I walk over to the cooler and there are two or three Latinos speaking. They stop talking about what they were talking about and they quickly change the subject. They greet me, but I can tell they did not want me to know what they were talking. It makes me feel like they don't trust me."

Black male speaks. "The same thing happens to me when I go to the cooler."

"Anyone?"

A male officer responds. "I'll speak for myself. But I know it's for the others as well. I stop talking because we are usually talking about our families, our parties, or our children's birthdays or celebrations. I stop because I have heard people make fun of our religious holidays like Day of the Dead or how much money we spend on quincineros for our daughters or how many people we have living together under one roof. I don't want to hear that shit anymore. I am tired of it, so I stop. Maybe it's wrong of me or us to do that, but none of us ever get asked about our families, our children, parents, or grandparents. At least I haven't."

"I'm not sure we have enough time to get to the other example of 'talking louder' or to the one about the white officers perceived as racist. I would like to spend the rest of our time today on these two examples and what anyone is willing to do to address these issues—issues that make us less trustworthy and cooperative. And

I'm sure these are affecting your being able to do a better job in the field. Please make it short. A sentence will suffice. Please start your sentence with the phrase 'I am willing to.'"

"I am willing to stop telling jokes about welfare or jokes about any people of color since I realize that many will not find them funny but will find them offensive."

"I am willing to greet people who walk over to the water cooler and inform them of what we are talking about regardless of the subject."

"And I will respect what you are talking about, and since I have been asking personal questions about your life, and getting to know you a bit, I may even be aware of what you are already discussing."

"Those are all excellent. Your homework for our last training is to think about how these issues that you brought in today about your relationships to each other have affected your work with the communities you serve. Thank you for your participation, and we will see you soon. You are dismissed. Have a good rest of the day."

"That was something, boss. They really got into it. I was impressed."

"Yes, Pat. And that they could see what they were doing and acknowledge it should make it much easier for them to see the connections between what they do in the precinct and what they do in the field."

CHAPTER 9

"Mr. and Mrs. Marshall, thanks for seeing us on such a short notice. I'm Detective Porter and this is Detective Caine. Were here to follow up with a few more questions about the murder of your son-in-law."

"We told the other officers everything we know."

"Yes, we are aware of that, but we have some more questions. Would you mind talking with us?'

"Not at all, Detective. We have nothing to hide. Do I detect a bit of a drawl, which I think is similar to ours?"

"Yes, sir. I left West Virginia when I was young, about eleven, but when I come around people who I grew up with, I just fall back into talking the way I used to."

"I think our families knew each other. Did you father work in the mine?"

"Yes, he did. Didn't everybody's?"

"Rob Porter? Oh my God. He and I used to go squirrel hunting. He said I was the best shot in town, but he was pretty damn good himself. We loved competing with each other for who would make the most kills. How is he?"

"He passed about two years ago. The mining got to him just like it got to everybody who worked there. Damn company would never take responsibility for anything. He told me about a big strike they were having. The company did not give an inch and outlasted the strikers. Broke their backs. He went back to work with less pay."

"Shame. Sorry to hear he passed."

"Thank you. We need to ask the two of you questions. You made a call to Saul Slater on the morning he was shot. Why was he calling you and what was said?"

Mrs. Marshall responds. "I called, Detective. I was just being respectful. When someone passes in West Virginia, we always call or drop in to show our respect, even if we don't like them. I knew it was his father and it seemed like a friendly thing to do."

"Were you planning to call the other Slater children?"

"I was, Detective. I think it just slipped my mind."

"Would you be willing to let us see your phone to see who else you have received phone calls from or have been calling?"

"Absolutely not. If we are under suspicion, you can get a warrant. Until then, I will protect my right to privacy. That's something, Detective Porter, you know, we Tennessee folk learn to do from an early age on. We don't like government interference. It usually ends up with our losing money, or land, or our homes. They took away our right to hunt for our own food and to make our own whiskey. I don't think I have anything to gain by cooperating with you since it has always been that we end up losing."

"This would not involve your losing anything. But it could help in the solving the case, solving who murdered Christina's husband."

"As my wife just said and I said earlier, we don't see how our private life could at all help you. We are not suspects and whom we speak to and call is our business. I have already spoken to you and cooperated about a private call. Nothing further needs to be discussed. And as we say in West Virginia, 'we thank you for your visit and hope the rest of the day goes well.'"

"Thank you both. And we also hope the rest of the day goes well for the both of you."

Caine speaks. "I think we struck out. That was a nice thing that happened about your father and Marshall."

"I don't think we struck out. And that nice thing that was uncovered was that Marshall and my dad were on the same side of the picket line during the strike. For some reason, that I don't understand, they did not go squirrel hunting after the strike was ended or I should say broken, and I don't even think they spoke to each other anymore after that. Something must have happened between the two of them or between the wives."

"Do you see any relevance of that for our case?"

"Not now. But it may be. Bitterness between folks in West Virginia hardly ends with just that feeling. It usually lasts generations. Its been there for generations. There is ill will, and most people who lose loved ones think about revenge. And one thing I am sure of is back there, revenge is carried out, even if it has to be done to the next generation."

"Let's make sure we put that idea in the report when we report to Zuma later. That revenge notion sounds like a powerful idea and certainly enough of one for motive. Could be it is going on in the cases we have in front of us."

"Maybe we can squeeze in another interview before we head back to the office. We should call Belcher and Martin now and have them check to see if the other Slater kids received any calls of condolences from the Marshalls."

"Good idea. When we speak with Zuma, lets suggest that he should probably subpoena the Marshalls' phones. In that way we can find out who else in this town they are connected with. We need put a move on to get back in time for the other interviews."

—◦—

"Okay, people, lets settle down and listen to what each found out in the interviews and what thoughts you have for following up."

Caine spoke. "It was a smart to send Porter along. Marshall picked up the accent and spoke a lot about the past. He and Porter's father worked in the mines together and were on the same side during this bitter strike. Something happened, however, because these men who used to be friends and who went squirrel hunting, no longer spoke. There was a lot of bitterness in the town after the strike, and Porter says that bitterness lasts, and it lasts through generations."

"Yes, and revenge could easily be a motive in the cases we're working on now."

"Is it your impression that Marshall could be seeking revenge and if so, on who?"

Pat spoke. "Slater would not be a likely target for revenge. He wasn't from the South. One of his jealous frustrated directors might be seeking revenge. Do you think whatever happened between Marshall and your dad, Porter, might have been ought of a reason to target your dad? What did you say your dad died of?"

"The mines, Detective. He was one of hundreds killed by working the mines. Most of us knew at least three generations of our families who, day after day, usually seven days a week, mined away. I call it slaving away. We had to accept what it did to our families. It was pretty much the only way to make a living. We all grew up with the knowledge that West Virginia had one of the worst mining disasters in our country's history. It happened in 1907, believe it or not, our own town, Monogahlia. It was a shadow that hung over the town like the coal dust from the mines."

"Porter, this may seem like a weird time, but do you have any feelings of seeking revenge, and if so, whom?"

"I can't tell you how often I have wanted to do that. But to whom? If I took revenge on the owners by destroying the mine, I would be hurting the workers more than the owners. They slaved away, but it did keep food on the table, barely."

"Caine, what about the call on the phone?"

"Mrs. Marshall said that was just what people in West Virginia did when someone passes. Even though they didn't know the Saul kid, they assumed he was in grief. But we really don't know the nature of the call, except that it was initiated by the Marshalls."

"Alverez, what did you and Edwards find out? You spent your time going through the belongings of Alice Bourne?"

"Yes, boss. We checked her rolodex, an answering machine, her computer, and her mobile phone. The rolodex and the mobile showed that she knew at least two officers from the precinct you're doing the training with. The emails showed that there were at least four other directors, writer types, who were pissed off at Slater and one director who she was pissed off at. The answering machine showed three calls had been made from their precinct, none from ours."

"Make sure that the two of you follow up with the other director who was angry with Slater. Please do that as quickly as possible."

"Edwards, Alvarez, do you know any of your colleagues who knew or talked about Alice Bourne or who had contact with movie or TV people? I'm not asking you to squeal but just to say yes or no."

"No, sir. I never heard anyone talking about TV contracts or offers unless they were watching it the night before."

"Pat, we're going to have to interview officers about Bourne, but let's wait till after the training. We also need to interview the other director-writer friends that Alvarez and Edwards found on the rolodex. We don't have to wait for the training to be over. We can start that tomorrow. But I want the director who Bourne was fighting with to be interviewed ASAP."

"Belcher, Martin, how did the interview with the sibs go?"

"Nothing much. They are upset about the loss of their brother. They both are convinced that it was Mr. and Mrs. Marshall who did it. This would mean less money to be divided up if there was a court case. And they think it was a warning to them to not challenge the insurance settlement. They are not frightened and are planning to go ahead with a legal challenge and have already found a lawyer."

"All of you have done well. I think you can return to your precinct tomorrow. We're going to do the last day of training. I assume you will have other assignments while we're finishing up our work at your shop. I will be writing a letter of recommendation for each of you and ask that it be put in your files. Thank you, see you tomorrow."

CHAPTER 10

Pat knew that Zuma was in a contemplative mood as they headed for the training. His toothpick which had come out of his shirt pocket, was in his mouth, and he was reciting the words. "The answer my friend is blowin' in the wind."

The call came in from Thompson. He was furious.

"Zuma, two of my officers have been shot. Both were in the training you were doing. I think we should call it off. Do you think it had anything to do with what they had talked about in the training?"

"First, let's not call the training off. I want to meet with them to discuss what has happened. I don't think it has to do with anything that happened in the training, but you can never tell. We will know a lot more after we meet. Try and separate the rest of your officers from our meeting. If you want, you can talk with your other officers. Maybe they will have some ideas of why or whom. We can talk after today's training. I hope you can let me do what I think is best for your officers and even for our case."

"Zuma, I will agree and I will wait."

"Who were the officers who were shot?"

"One was the only Latina in your group, Sandra Sanchez, and the other was Gerald Knox."

"Did they survive? How were they shot?"

"I assume they might have been an item. They were coming out of her home early this morning and a shooter from across the street got off two rounds before they each hit the ground. One witness said he saw a car about fifty yards away taking off right after he heard the shots. The bullets each came close to their hearts. This was one hell of a shooter. They're both critical right now. The witness could not get a plate on the car. It was still pretty dark out at six thirty. Thinks the car was a dark one either brown or black."

"Thanks, Chief. We should be there in about ten minutes."

"We're not going to do our training today. We have had a tragedy. I know there are many, if not all of you, are upset. Even if you did not know or were not close with Officers Sanchez or Knox it is more than an attack on them personally, it is an attack on your precinct and the police officers in this city. They were shot early this morning, leaving the Sanchez home. They were together. At this point, Chief Thompson says they are both in critical but stable condition. The doctors feel the prognosis is good. So, let's talk about how we feel."

"That's bullshit, Detective Zuma. I respect you, but I don't think we should waste time and talk about our feelings. We're all upset. I think we should be putting as many officers into the field and find the sons of bitches who did this."

"I think going into the field is a good idea, but I think we have to start a little closer to home. Sanchez and Knox were in the training we all did together."

There is as long silence.

"Detective Zuma, are you suggesting that someone in our training shot them?"

"I don't know who shot them. I do know lots of strong feelings emerge whenever we do this kind of work."

"I'm willing to account for the time when Knox and Sanchez were shot. I woke at six to get here for our training. I had a bite with my wife and headed straight here. My wife can verify the time I left. Maybe everyone else can do the same."

"Instead of each person here reporting on their whereabouts this morning, can you each write down where you were between six and seven thirty and whom we might contact to confirm this? If any of you do not wish to do this, please indicate that you are not willing. Pat, can you please collect their notes. I'd like to go back and address the feelings we had from yesterday's training."

"I was pretty upset to hear that the Latinos did not trust me. Even though I said I would not take it personally, I knew that I left with hurt and even angry feelings."

"I was angry, too, but I don't think I would ever take it to the point that I would shoot my fellow officer."

"I left pretty steamed about not getting to talk about what I see as the racism I receive among other whites in the department."

Pat speaks. "Did you discuss that with any of the other officers or anyone else outside the department?"

"Yeah, walking out, Healey came over and said he had put the same thing down and thanked me for speaking up."

"Officer Healey, would you care to comment?"

"I did make that comment because I was steamed. But a white officer, Martin, and a Latina were shot. If I were the shooter, why would I want to shoot a fellow white officer? As far as being angry at the Latinos, I have a witness who can verify where I was this morning."

"I don't think there is anything more to discover here regarding the suspects for the shooting. We will be checking the statements you handed in verifying your whereabouts. If you mentioned a witness, please do not speak to them. We will be notifying them. Please don't tell them to expect a call. On the way out, I'd like you to allow us to check your phones to see the calls made over the last two days up until this morning when you arrived. I know this could be considered an invasion of privacy, but I hope you understand that it allows us to move forward on the shooting. If you object, tell Pat on the way out. If there are no more comments, we can end our meeting today. We will have to have one more training session, but I think we might have to wait few days to allow us to verify your statements and to pursue the Sanchez and Martin shootings."

"Chief Thompson, I'd like your staff to follow up the reports that the officers handed in. Can you use officers who weren't in the training? It shouldn't take a lot of time."

"We can do that, Zuma. I'll get on it this afternoon. You might have all the information by tomorrow. Do you have any suggestions about what else I might be doing or we can do together about our officer shootings? The press is screaming. They're crying about a police officer rampage. The public is afraid also. My office is getting calls with people saying if police officers are not safe, how they be safe. They want to know what we are planning to do. I'm not surprised. It's what I would expect them to feel."

"We're just going to have them scream. You can make the usual statement about leads being followed up and anyone having information about that type of car. Pat and I have to follow up with some things about the Slater case. You can check the pictures that Pat has taken of your officers' phones to see if any were made to any of the suspects in the Slater case or to each other. If one of them refused to allow Pat to take a picture, could you personally call them? I know this is treading on dangerous grounds as the union might be pissed, but we are legally allowed to subpoena in cases where we think a suspect is involved. It will be hard to show why anyone who refuses to let us see his or her phone is a suspect, but you can try. I'm sure they would rather want to stay in your good graces than be seen as defending a principle. We'll win in the end, but it will be a long time if they don't cooperate."

"Zuma, do you think the shot officers were the result of the training or are connected to the Slater case?"

"Chief Thompson, I think the Slater case is definitely connected to the shootings. I'm not sure if the training is, but if it is, it would be more indirectly related. And by indirect, I mean there might be missing links between the training, the shot officers, and Slater's murder. I would also like you to check the files of each officer in the training and find out where they were born. If any of them come from West Virginia, please get back to me immediately."

"Can you explain or speculate?"

"No, the ideas are too fuzzy for me to talk about."

On the way back to Santa Monica, Pat saw the toothpick come out of the pocket and knew that humming would soon follow.

"Boss, that was quite a wild speculation. I guess I will have to wait till your thoughts become less fuzzy."

"I think they will sharpen when we go back and do some more interviews."

Zuma began humming. Pat said the words in his head while Zuma hummed. He liked that he could say the words at the same time as Zuma hummed each bar. Zuma smiled and continued to hum as Pat began to sing the words, "The answer my friend is blowin' in the wind, the answer is blowin' in the wind."

He was looking foward to going home and happy to be able to go over things with Claudia.

❦

"It's always messier, Claudia, when one of our own gets shot, but even worse, if the suspect might also be one of our own."

"How many suspects do you have, Joe?"

"More than I have ever had before. Even when there is a murder in an apartment, there aren't that many tenants. In this case, we have the ones from the Slater murder, the officers from the training, and with possibly a larger number from the precinct. It's not like we have to interview them all. But each of them might lead to another suspect. We have a lot of groundwork checking phones and verifying schedules. It's muddy right now, but the waters will clear with some good old-fashioned police work, and we'll see a few of the fish more clearly."

"Joe, I'm always reminded of how much your work is like mine. When I first start a painting, especially if I'm doing it from memory, things are also muddy. I have the big picture but can't see the details clearly. And as I slowly work on one aspect of my painting and even get one detail, other details come into focus and are clear."

"Your work sounds creative, darling. Mine is just old-fashioned grunt work. It's digging out the rocks and mud that don't belong to get to the fish the ones you need to dig into."

"Let's go out and eat, Joe, and when we get home, you can dig into me."

Joe laughed. "I can dig that idea, darling. It will be nice, easy, and sweet because with you there is never a lot of mud or stones to deal with. Your waters are never muddy. They are clear and allow me to admire you and see deeply."

It was Claudia's turn to laugh. "And I love that you see and admire all my details."

On the way to dinner, Joe began singing the song about the place where they fell in love. He had played it for Claudia, shortly after she had decided to come and live with him in Santa Monica. He sang the words about sand dunes, salty air and lobster stew alone but when it came to the last phrase of "Old Cape Cod," they sang in unison.

"You're sure to fall in love, in love, with old Cape Cod…"

CHAPTER 11

"I need some of you to keep working on the Slater case today even though some of our own have been shot. Martinez and Ball, follow up with those four director-writer folks who were listed in the rolodex and on her phone—when did they last meet and had they ever talked about doing anything to Slater. Stress the idea of their talking so they won't be suspicious. Let's get this done by today."

"Boss, did you have anything in mind for us? Thompson said that one person refused to let us see his phone. Everyone has provided the names of a witness to verify their whereabouts. Even Mr. No Phone."

"Pat, you and I are going to check with Chief Thompson first and ask him if we can interview his officers who were at the desk when Alice Bourne made her calls. We can tell them we need to know about the nature of their relationship to her and what the calls were about."

"What if they ask for a lawyer or a union rep?"

"Then, we will honor it."

"Zuma, I'm fine with these interviews you propose. I think I should speak to them first and tell them we need to know more about Alice Bourne. I'll introduce you since the don't know you. They were not in the training."

"Let's have them in separate rooms. I'll take one and Pat can do the other."

"Okay. Let me call Robertson and Bailey in."

"Detective Robertson, can you tell me how long you knew Alice Bourne and what was the nature of your relationship?"

"I will be happy to tell you all that I know about her, but I will ask you to keep some of this confidential. I am married and I have two kids. Alice and I were lovers."

"I will respect that part of your story that involves your liaison with Ms. Bourne."

"I met her when I was called in on a brawl that was taking place in a bar. She had gone to a bar with some of her friends who were also writers and in the biz and had gotten pretty plastered. She was accusing everyone in the place of being afraid to fight for their rights. This was directed at total strangers and her friends. She had thrown a few punches and even though she was screaming and seemed totally out of control, she was able to land a few solid wallops. I guess she had been into some martial arts. The bartender issued the call, and I showed up along with Bailey. No one wanted to press charges, and she and I chatted about what she was angry about."

"What did she say?"

"She cursed at the way in which the cards were stacked against women in the business. She said she left West Virginia to get away from the oppression of men but found that it was as bad or even worse here in LA. While she was talking, Bailey had made sure that no one wanted medical care. That was the beginning of our relationship."

"How long were you involved?"

"Well, it was about three months. She knew I was married and wanted more. I did not. We stayed friends."

"What was the nature of the call you made to her the day before Saul Slater was killed?"

"I wanted to tell her that her old nemesis, the guy she disliked so much who called her a loser and who would never help her, had been shot and she should be happy."

"Was she?"

"Alice was not the kind of woman who could be happy. Growing up in the South, she had to deal with a lot of peckers who were only into her tail. She left West Virginia early, but she felt that even the men up here were out to rob her of her place in the world."

"Was she surprised to hear that Slater had been shot?"

"I don't exactly recall, but I don't think she was surprised."

"Did she ever discuss with you how revenge was a big factor in people's relationships in West Virginia and how it could last for generations?"

"Yes, she did. She said if she could be sure she could get away with murder, there were a few people she would like to do away with."

"Any names?"

"No, Detective Zuma. Can't help you with that."

"Is there anything that you did with her that was of help to her?"

"I did help her out a few times with her rent. This was after we broke up. I couldn't give much. My wife and I have three kids."

"Did you know that Alice was a good shot?"

"Well, yes, I did as a matter of fact. I snuck her into our practice range, and I was shocked at how well that woman could shoot. She outshot me, and I'm pretty good with a gun. She told me that everyone learned to shoot in the town. When they grow up, it's a way for families to get food, so everyone learns to start shooting at a young age."

"Do you know where she got her gun?"

"No, she had it the night I met her. She showed it to me in her glove compartment."

"And what was her relationship to your fellow detective, Detective Bailey?"

"You're going to have to ask him about that, which is what I assume is going on in the other room right now."

"Thanks, Detective. I think were finished."

"I hope that what I told you about Alice will not be revealed to my wife. I want to keep my marriage. But I would really like your word on it."

"No problem with that."

On the way back, Pat told Zuma what he had found out about Bailey and Bourne.

"They were lovers, boss."

"Wow. Pat, you must be familiar with the song that has the refrain, 'Go ask Alice when she's ten feet tall.'"

"No, boss."

"Well, our Alice Bourne was a biggie. Someone would have to be strong and confident to take her on. Robertson was also her lover and she could outshoot any of them. The song is about drug addiction. It was a way to talk about drugs and got past the censors. Not important about this case, but a great song. The words make me think of Ms. Bourne as big, strong, confident, and, yes, ten feet tall."

"Thanks, boss, I'll find it and listen."

"I think she must have some impact and connection to these police shootings and maybe to Slater."

"Any ideas on how, boss?"

"Let's find out who else in the precinct was from West Virginia. And I was thinking…" Zuma pulled the toothpick out of his left shirt pocket, placed it in his mouth, and started humming. "Did anyone ever identify the body we got from Slater's apartment as actually being Alice Bourne?"

"No, boss. We asked Christina to come down and identify it but she said she was too upset."

"Well, Pat, maybe Alice Bourne is ten feet tall. And more importantly, maybe she is still alive. And if she is, she will not be able to hide for very long. We need to check the supposed Bourne body and run prints on it and see if it's in our database. Also, let's check the missing persons reports starting with three days after Slater was killed. If it wasn't Bourne, then someone who knew the vic, her, parents, friends, or roommates would report her missing. We need to do that quickly. If the body wasn't Bourne's, we have a new ball game."

"I'm on it, boss."

Pat found a missing person's report for a Cynthia Goodling. When he Googled her name, he found out that she, like Alice Bourne, was an assistant director.

"Boss, you were right to be suspicious. Alice Bourne is not dead."

"I'm sure she is more than ten feet tall."

"Boss, those people from west Virgina keep showing up. Chief Thompson found that there were two men in his precinct who were also born in West Virginia. Neither of the names he gave me, LaSalle and Granger were in our training."

"Let's check with the chief and see if he would be okay if we interview them. If he's on board with this, let him make the call so they know it's from the top."

—m—

"Mr. LaSalle, Mr. Granger, thank you for coming in. Detectives, my chief assistant Detective Vasquez and I are investigating the murder of Richard Slater and his son Saul Slater." Zuma had decided not to mention Alice Bourne.

LaSalle spoke, "Chief never said what it was for. How can we help you with these other murders? We weren't on the case. They were in your precinct."

"Of course. We were interested in the fact that you were both born in West Virginia. The girlfriend of Richard Slater was also born in the same state. We were wondering if you knew her or the family?"

Granger laughed and spoke.

"West Virginia is not a big state, Detective, but the mountains make it bigger than it is in actual area since it takes a while to get around the state. Northerners treat it like it's a small town. They also think and we marry each other, cousins marrying cousins, and parents marrying nieces or nephews, and if we're not marrying, were making our own booze, getting drunk, and hunting. But you're in luck, we all do come from a small town, and I knew my buddy's family and the Marshall family growing up. And all our parents knew each other. We did make our own booze and hunt. We didn't marry each other, but the mine connected us all."

"And how did the mine connect you? Did you all work underground? Were any members of the family's foreman?"

"I can't recall who was a foreman or not, but we all knew the names of the folks who didn't walk the picket line with us. I think there were seven miners who didn't strike with us."

"So, what happened to the families when the strike was broken."

"Different things. There was a lot of bitterness even between people who had picketed together. The company brought in blacks, and some families hated the blacks, others didn't and blamed the company. Strikers even began blaming each other for whether that had or had not voted to go on strike. It drove us all to different corners. My family didn't like it that blacks were being blamed and my dad decided to leave. We pulled up stakes from a town that he and his grandfather had been raised in. It was tough on him and tough on my Ma. She had lots of friends, and coming to Los Angeles uprooted both of them."

"My family and the Grangers also left. It was really hard for us to pull up stakes, but my dad was absolutely convinced that the company was going to get worse after the strike. He kept repeating over and over that they were going to lower wages and increase prices at the company-owned stores in town."

"Our families, the Grangers and LaSalles, became closer once we got to LA. George and I both decided we wanted to be cops."

"Wait a second, buddy. I was the one who convinced Robert to join up and apply to the academy. I think it was a way for both of us to believe we could fight for fairness and to support families."

"Do you know that Alice Bourne is missing?"

Robert Lasalle and George Granger looked at each other with a look of "aha."

"We were just talking about her this morning. We hadn't heard from Alice lately. She usually calls ever few days. How long has she been missing?"

"About ten days. What were her calls about?"

Nothing special. I think those West Virginia blue ridge mountain bonds kept us together. We could always share how different things were up here. We reminisced about missing hunting together and tasting homemade booze. She would also talk about her work and how it was harder here up north than in West Virginia for a woman. She would say often say that in the South, you knew who opposed you but here in the north, men smile and are friendly but could never be trusted to support you."

"Did she ever talk about anyone that she disliked?"

"She never mentioned names."

"Detective Zuma, are you thinking that Alice had something to do with the Slater killing?"

"Yes, we are thinking that is a possibility. If you hear from her, please let us know."

"We sure will, but I can't imagine Alice being that angry that she would murder. She has lived with frustration for a long, long time. It's something we all grow up with in West Virdgina— frustration over no pay checks, no food for a day or so, or no Christmas presents. It was a way of life for us."

"I'm sorry that it was that way for the two of you and others. Hopefully, things have improved down there and hopefully, you're right about Bourne not being capable of murder. Thank you both, and please call if you speak to or hear from Alice. Also, I know it's a lot to ask but since this is an investigation, I hope your loyalty to the department and the case will overcome your loyalty to her and not mention that we questioned you or are looking for her."

"We can do that, Detective."

"What do you think, Pat?"

"They seem like straight shooters about their past, boss, but I think they were protective of the Bourne woman. I don't know what they know, but I don't think they only talked about the good old days of boozemaking, hunting, and Alice's frustration. I think that strike did something to change them and bind them together in different ways. I think those bonds are probably stronger than the ones they feel towards the department or the case."

"Let's tell Thompson we need to put an observer at each of their homes. We don't want any changes in the station and their work. If they have something to hide, they will be extra cautious. We don't want to tip our hand. We need twenty-four-hour observation for both of them. He may not want to put his own staff observing their own people, so he may ask us to do it. He may also want Internal Affairs in his own precinct handling it. We need to do this quickly. If they have something to hide, they will be moving quickly also."

CHAPTER 12

"Joe, I found a studio and have signed a lease. It's a small space upstairs on the 3rd Street mall. I don't have to do much to set it up. It has fresh paint and a window facing the mall so that passersby will be able to see what I hang in the window."

"Congratulations. How can I help? If you're there during the days, when will you have time for your teaching and painting?"

I'm going to get some art students from UCLA, USC, and Santa Monica City college. They will be able to receive academic credit as I will be talking and critiquing their work. The schools consider this an internship. They'll have a desk they can use to study, and I'll have an extra easel or two for them to paint. I don't think I will need much help from you. We can load up ten or so paintings in the car and carry them over. I want the students to be involved with hanging them."

"You are amazing. I think that the tourists who go through the mall would be happy to see your landscapes of the Pacific and purchase so they can bring one home to have a memory. It's marketing without having to advertise. The window with your landscapes is your advertisement. I think there will probably be well over a thousand people a day who will probably see your work. How very clever."

"And I can set it up so the students don't have to handle cash. Purchases will all be done with a credit card."

"This definitely calls for a celebration. Do you want to do it tonight or wait until the studio is set up?"

"Let's wait till we get all the work done. Maybe we can even take the interns out. It feels like I will be teaching more dedicated and more mature students than what I do now at SafePaths."

At the mention of SafePaths, Zuma stopped thinking about the new studio, the interns, the crowds who would be seeing his wife's work and how he was going to help Claudia. All thoughts of celebration disappeared. They were replaced by the focus he had had about the woman he was convinced had murdered her husband. He shuddered as he thought about the intense discussions and disagreements he had with Claudia over the suspected murderer who had a child, Lucy, at the school Claudia was teaching in. She had grown very fond of the child and she and Joe had battled over Joe's pursuit of the case.

"You can't go after her. If you get solid evidence and she is convicted, what will happen to Lucy? There is no one else in the family who would be able to take care of her. She will be handed over to foster care. And she's now a kid whose mother is a murderer. Other kids will chew her up and make mincemeat of her. She will be hounded and humiliated. That's too much for any child to handle. She has lost a father, a teacher, and now could lose her mother. Joe, you need to have mercy on this kid."

"Claudia, I wish I could. I've taken an oath. I've sworn to search for the guilty. That is my job. That is what I do. I am there to ensure that the scales of justice are balanced. Murderers can't just walk around scot-free."

"You need to put mercy on those scales of justice, Joe. This is not like you. This is not your best self. Your suspected murderer, the mother, has already lived two years scot-free. You haven't solved the other crime that you believe she is guilty of. What is wrong with her having more years? Not every crime is solved."

Joe had never been confronted with anything like this in all the years he had been a detective. Someone was asking him to not pursue someone who was probably guilty. If this were a higher up, even if was the mayor, he would refuse to accept that directive. But this was Claudia, the woman he loved. He was torn.

"Joe, if you go forward, I will seek to adopt her. If she comes into our life, she will never accept you. She will come between us. Please don't do this. She is an innocent. She is not an innocent adult who is falsely

accused and called names but who can fight back and can understand reasons for people's animosity. She is an innocent child. A most innocent child."

"Claudia, you're making me choose between you and my integrity."

"In my eyes, you would have more integrity if you give up your pursuit. You will lose integrity in my eyes if you pursue the case. Your integrity will only increase if you include mercy as part of the reasoning to drop your pursuit."

He was not sleeping well and was irritable and short with Claudia. She was patient with him, realizing how difficult it was for him to have seen the world through the eyes of a child rather than through his career eyes. She marveled that he was able to keep wrestling with the issue of whether he had done right or wrong.

"Joe, remember when you told me how angry you were that your wife got killed. Suppose you had done something in revenge and you were sent away, what do you think that would have done to your children, knowing that their father murdered someone?"

"I can only imagine. It would have been horrendous. It probably would have wrecked their lives."

"Yes, and you would have been haunted by the idea of what you had done to your children. I believe that Sonia must sometimes feel the same way."

"Maybe you're right. I wish I knew that."

"Your guilty party, Lucy's mother, did something out of revenge, revenge on a cheating husband. What you're doing now is preventing a life from being wrecked."

Joe realized that he and Claudia had locked horns. He was finding it hard to move and change the feelings he had about the oath he took and his commitment to bring to justice all of those whose crimes were clear.

That last comment helped Joe change in his basic beliefs about justice. Claudia and Joe both knew that he changed because of her. He now saw more of the world as she did made her feel close to him in a way that she never realized was possible. Joe knew that what felt at first like giving up something was in fact a set of gains. He had gained a view of mercy, a view of the world as a child sees it. He had also gained the surety that addition of mercy to his pursuit of justice had created a bond between them that would never be broken.

He had avoided asking about Sonia or her daughter but now decided it was better to know.

"Claudia, please fill me in on the details that you know I have not asked you about and that you have astutely avoided telling me."

"The child is blossoming. She gets great grades on all her academic subjects and her woodworking skills are astounding. Sonia has been volunteering at a halfway house for battered women. She teaches them woodworking and coleads a group based on their twelve-step program. I think she must have taken the steps seriously because she has been talking about her character defects with me on her visits to SafePaths when she picks her up."

"I hope she does not include me when she gets to apologies for those she lied to. If she tries to, I'm not sure I would want to hear definite proof of what she did. It might make me do something that I know would not be good for us. I hope its past the statute of limitations so I would not be tempted or haunted."

"Joe, I hope it would be also, I would not want you to be haunted. I think you need to know that you did a good thing. You need to hold on to that. We just can never know what will happen in life. You may have let a guilty party go, but by doing that you have allowed a lot more good to happen in the world—good that would have never happened if you did not have mercy."

"That's true, darling, except I do know what will happen in our world. Our love will continue to happen in our lives together."

The call came in as Zuma and Claudia we're finishing up dinner. It was from Pat.

"Boss, sorry to interrupt, but I just got a call about those two West Virginia boys. Our men observing each one of them said they left their residences and they met at a bar. It just looked it was going to be a routine evening of cops sitting around drinking and shooting the breeze. After about ten minutes, a woman walked in and sat down with them. Our guys called and wanted to know what to do. Should they walk up and get an ID on the woman or wait to see who leaves with whom but make sure to follow the woman? And while we were talking, another male walked in. Much older. What do you suggest they do, boss?"

"Make sure that one of them follows the woman and the other follow the older man. Even though we know where those West Virginia boys live, if we can, we want to make sure where they go. You'll have to call in for two more officers. If they don't get there in time and the party leaves, make sure that at least the woman and the older man are followed. Thanks, Pat, for keeping me up to date."

When Zuma arrived in the morning, he found the report that the observers had lost their suspects.

"The woman must've known she was being followed and she was really good at alluding the tail. Same with the older guy. They each left with one of the West Virginia boys. We don't know where they went."

"Pat, we got some real pros here. We're going to have to figure out what could tie them together."

At that moment, a call came in from the field.

"Zuma, this is Thompson. We found a body dumped off the 4th Street Bridge. I think you should come down and take a look. We haven't touched anything."

"I'm leaving now."

On the way into LA, another call came in from the field.

"Detective, we just found a body at the bottom of the bluffs in Santa Monica. Could be a suicide, but I'm waiting for some backup. It's caused a big traffic mess."

"I'm going to stop my driving and let Pat Vasquez pick up an Uber and get there ASAP. Don't touch anything. Rope off the area and try to keep the traffic from moving. Also get someone on the bluffs so that the lookie-loos don't get close to the edge and fall off. All that rain mush have softened the soil. Pat, keep me in touch."

"Boss, these two couldn't be related. And could they possibly be related to our Slater case?"

"I don't know, Pat. If we have pros at work, they would make things look as unrelated as possible. Get going and call your Uber. I want you to be in complete charge of the mess on the bluffs. I trust you to preserve the scene."

CHAPTER 13

Zuma and Thompson were conferring at some distance away from the other officers. They spoke softly and each agreed that it had not been a suicide. The man's neck had been first broken and then tossed off the bridge. There was no theft involved as he still had his wallet in the rear pocket. A closed button had prevented it from falling out during the fall. The contents revealed that he was a bookkeeper in a law firm close to downtown. Zuma recognized the law firm and knew it to be prestigious. The name on the law firm card was Alvin Roman. There were pictures of the victim along with, what Zuma assumed to be, a spouse and two children in their teens.

"Zuma, we're going to check the neck for fingerprints."

"I don't think you'll find any. It looks like a pro job—someone strong and probably wore gloves—but go ahead."

"Zuma, I've got to tell you. At first when I got the call, I thought it might be another one of my officers. I can't believe it, but I was relieved about finding a murder victim that I didn't know. I'll get the body to the morgue. We need to go to the home address and call the law firm and do some interviewing there and the home. Pictures look like the guy was married and had kids."

"I know what you mean about the relief, but I am suspicious that this might be related to our ongoing investigation of the other murders and I would..."

The call came in from Pat.

"Boss, definitely not a suicide."

"Let me guess, Pat. The man's neck was broken and there are no fingerprints. There was a wallet on the body so he could be identified."

"Boss, how in God's name would you know all that? And we did identify him. He lives in our precinct and has a family. He works in a local market where it says he is a manager. Name is Scott Haskin."

"Pat, you take charge of the body, notify the family and the workplace. Get any help you need."

"Thompson, we have mirror images of the murders, and we are engaged in a mirror image of the two investigations that your staff and my staff will be doing."

"Zuma, if I ever hear police work is boring, I will crack their skulls. This is Sherlock Holmes kind of stuff. Sherlock had the London fog and you have your Santa Monica fog. Do you think we could write about this? The props look good—a bridge, bluffs, fog, and similar murders."

"And I think we shall discover that my foggy murder and your fogless murder will be connected. And since I know we are as good as Sherlock, we shall discover how these two murders are related to our ongoing investigations.'

"I think your stretching it, Zuma."

"I am stretching it, but that's what our pros are doing. They are organized and clever and would seem to do everything they can to throw us off their trail."

"Okay, Sherlock, lead the way. I'm happy to be Watson."

"But I don't think I would waste my time writing about this murder mystery. I'm going to do a real-world interview now."

<hr>

"Detective Bailey, can you tell me who you were with in the bar last night? We know you were with a lady."

"Sure, Detective. It was Alice Bourne."

Zuma smiled. That song was getting to be more and more accurate in describing Alice Bourne. "I thought you were going to let me know as soon as you heard from her."

"I did make that promise to you, and I was planning to keep it. She showed up at the bar and was with me all night. I just never had an opportunity to call you, and I didn't want to do that in front of her."

"So, you're seeing her again."

"I wouldn't say that. She just showed up."

"How did she know you were there?"

"I'm not sure. Alice is pretty smart. If she wants something, she figures out what to do. She may have been following me."

"You say you spent the night together, I don't suppose that anyone can verify that."

"No, Detective Zuma, no one can. You're just going to have to take my word."

"Can you give me an address for Bourne?"

"I wish I could, but she didn't give it to me when I asked her for it."

"We struck out, Pat, but we're going to score eventually. Let's put a tail on Bailey at his residence so that in case our lady of the evening shows, we're there. We also need to follow him when he leaves the station in case he might be meeting up with her. If we see her with him, we go up and say we have a warrant to bring her down to the station, and that should do it. What did you find out when you interviewed Detective Robertson?"

"Boss, the old man was Mr. Marshall. They said they were just getting together like they occasionally do to talk about the good all days and that he drove him home."

"And I'm sure Mrs. Marshall will vouch for whatever time he says he got home. I believe we need to put tail on Mr. Marshall and Detectives Granger, LaSalle, Bailey, and Robertson. We need a twenty-four-hour tail on Marshall, and we need to a tail on the two detectives, Bailey and Robertson. We need to know what they do from the moment they leave work until they show up at work the following morning."

Zuma hoped that a close overnight watch would prove to be sucessful.

"Zuma, we hit a patch of luck. Bourne was picked up this morning as she was knocking on Belcher's door. I have her in the station now. I think I should be questioning her but would like you to come down and be ready in case I strike out. She has called her lawyer, a guy named Silverberg."

Zuma recognized the name and knew that Irving Silverberg had done this many times for the folks who came from West Virginia. He had been called in to defend the strikers' right to picket and even though the strike was broken and the case never got to court, he had continued defending the strikers and their families through the years.

"I'm on my way."

"Chief Thompson, as I told the other detective, there is no evidence that has been established linking my client to a case. Why is she being harassed?"

"She showed up at a suspect's home and has often been seen with him. We wanted to bring her in for some further questioning."

"I will sit with her and provide advice."

When Zuma entered the room, Silverberg spoke. Oddly, he seemed to be speaking more to Zuma than to Thompson.

"Detective Zuma, Chief Thompson, I have spoked with my client and she has told me you want to know some things about her personal life, like her dating life and the names of friends. I have advised her she need not to talk unless you have cause to show the relevance of your questions to a case you are pursuing."

"She is a suspect, and I am going to ask for a court order restraining her from leaving the state."

"I will have to contest that. You will have to convince the court as to why she is a suspect."

"Thank you, Mr. Silverberg. As you probably often have said, 'see you in court.'"

At that moment, Zuma turned to Thompson and called him outside.

"I'd like to take this, if you don't mind. I've got a feeling about how I might get to her to reveal something."

"I have absolutely no problem with that."

"Mr. Silverberg, I would like a few more moments with Ms. Bourne."

"That is up to her. My advice is that we leave."

"Let's stay for a few moments, Irving."

"Ms. Bourne, I would appreciate it if you could tell us a little bit about your growing up in West Virginia."

"Alice, that's a personal question that I advised you about. You don't have to answer."

"That's all right, Irv. It's not too often that a northerner is interested in us southerners. And this is a Northern male interested in a poor little old southern belle me. I'm rightly flattered, Detective Zuma,"

"Thank you, Ms. Bourne. Did you grow up poor?"

"Yes, Detective. I'm just the poor daughter of a poor coal miner."

"Oh, you're just like Loretta Lynn."

"Detective Zuma, I didn't realize you knew much about our southern culture. Yes, you might say I am Loretta Lynn's adopted sister. I have adopted her and that's because when she sings, she's talking about my life. Do you know the words I'm thinking of? I'll sing the words she sings that describe my life.

"I was borne a coal miner's daughter
In a cabin, on a hill in Butcher Holler
We were poor, but we had love
That's one thing that daddy made sure of."

Zuma interrupts and he starts to sing with her.

"He shoveled coal to make a poor man's dollar.
He worked all night in the Van Lear coal mines.
All day long in the field a hoin' corn."

"Detective Zuma, I'm very impressed with you."

"And wasn't the company that ran the mine in the town you were living also owned by Van Lear?"

"Yes, it was, Detective. That's another reason why I loved the song and Loreta and I are soul sisters."

"Ms. Bourne, I'm also thinking of the Tallahatchie Bridge song. Do you know that one?"

Zuma starts to sing again.

"Today, Billy Joe MacAllister jumped off the Tallahatchie Bridge
And papa said to mama, as he passed around the black-eyed peas
Well, Billy Joe never had a lick of sense; pass the biscuits, please.

"I got some news this morning, Ms. Bourne, that reminded me of that song. It looks like someone jumped off the bluffs in Santa Monica. Not exactly the Tallahatchie Bridge, but it did make me think of the similarity."

"Well it's a sad, sad world, Detective. I'm sure you know that better than I do."

"Yes, it is. There is a great song for that also. Do you know which one I'm thinking of?"

The lawyer interrupts. "This is not at all relevant, Detective. Alice, I think you should stop indulging Detective Zuma's perchance for songs and singing. Please let's end this interview right now."

"This is fun, Irving. I kind of like it. And I know a song that would be perfect. It's called "Somebody Done Somebody Wrong." The song is about one person hurting another and the sad and lonely feelings the wrong creates. The damn coal mine was doing wrong every damn day. It was belching smoke and putting its poison in the air for people to breathe. That's a big wrong, Detective, much bigger than any one person doing wrong to another."

"I got it, Ms. Bourne. And you're right, it is a much bigger wrong than the mine did than any one person could have done. But I would like to go back and talk about you. A lot of people have done you wrong, Alice, and a lot of other people have done a lot of other people wrong. And sometimes, it's a company. Sometimes, the wrongs hurt so bad that people seek revenge and sometimes they commit suicide. Do you know of anyone from your town who sought revenge or committed suicide?"

"I think all the folks who lost their jobs after the strike would have thought about revenge. I don't know if any of them did. I wouldn't blame them if they did. I don't know of any suicides."

"Thank you, Ms. Bourne. I enjoyed doing our little sing-a-long and you have been very helpful."

Alice knew a straight shooter when she met one, and she knew Zuma was telling her the truth about her being helpful. She couldn't understand how she had helped him. She was worried that she had given him some clues. She thought a question might help her figure out what she might have revealed to Zuma without being aware of what she had done.

"Detective, would you be willing to tell me your favorite song?"

"Sure, its 'Blowing in the Wind' Do you know it?"

"Yes, I do."

Alice didn't get what she was looking for, but she realized that Zuma had found something that was of value to him. She was stumped. She didn't want to give up.

"And would you have a second favorite?"

"It's a Beatles song, 'All You Need Is Love.'"

Now she was really stumped. How could this hard-nosed relentless detective who knows a world in which most people are doing other people wrong be a believer in love? She thought that if a BeAtles song was his second favorite it would be "Eleanore Rigby." That would be his song because she knew that Zuma's world must be full of "lonely people" with "nobody there and nobody cares." He definitely was not a coal miner's son.

—⚊—

"Alright Zuma, you may be Sherlock, but I failed as Watson. What do you think you found?"

"I think we may have found who is going to be next on the hit list. Let's go to your office."

"It must be the seven that you think is up next."

Zuma stopped in his tracks. How would Thompson know about the seven strikers? Why would he know that? He decided to not challenge the chief and responded nonchalantly.

"Good to have you on the Holmes-Watson team."

Zuma filed it as a question that had to be discovered.

CHAPTER 14

"Thompson, can we go into your library and let Pat pull up all the newspaper releases on the strike?"

It took about ten minutes before Pat asked the two to come over and read what he had found in his search.

"Wow we struck it rich. Here's the name of her lawyer."

Irving Silverberg to defend strikers in Tennessee.
Famous New York Lawyer to travel south
and Defend Strikers in Tennessee.
White miners cross picket line to join Black strike breakers
Violence erupts as White Miners throw rocks at
fellow Miners' who seek to keep mine running
The mining company of Van Elms facing violence inside
its own factory between white and black strike breakers

"Do any of the articles have the names of the strike breakers? If we can find those, I think we will find our past and our next victims."

"Here they are. It's an article after the strike was settled. Someone decided to do interviews with all the strike breakers. Many had already left town, but all the names are listed."

"How many are there, Pat?"

"Seven. Here they are: Al Roman, Scott Haskin, Dan Albertson, Mark Bittman, Phillip Copman, Mark Fitzgerald, and Leon Maxwell."

"Okay, two of those men, Roman and Haskin are dead. Roman was the supposed suicide on the bluffs and Haskin was the jumper from the 4th Street Bridge. I think there are more murders being planned. We need to get lookouts at the homes of each the people on the list who are still alive. We need twenty-four-hour surveillance. We also need to do interviews with every single one of them."

"Zuma, your singing worked wonders."

"Thank you, Thompson. Let's see if we get ahead of this rampage. There has got to be a leader in this revenge-seeking group. Someone has got to organize the timing of the hits. Maybe the strike people that we interview will have some ideas. I'm sure they know all the names of the people we know. I would imagine they might be running scared when they discover the names of the people who have been murdered or supposedly committed suicide. We need to get to them before they decide it would be better to leave town."

Zuma's cell phone rang and he recognized it immediately. He was surprised; it was from Claudia. It had to be important because she said she would not call during a workday unless it was critical.

"Honey, someone throw a rock in my gallery and broke the glass and then throw in a burning bottle with kerosene. Luckily, the alarm went off and there was not a lot of damage."

"Are you okay? Was anyone hurt?"

"No, it was early this morning before anyone had showed up. I got the call after the fire department had doused the flames."

"Where are you now?"

"I'm standing outside, looking up at the broken pane. I called for a replacement. It's good that I have insurance."

"Don't let them put the pane in till I get there. I'm on my way."

"Do you think we have gotten on that hit list, boss?"

"No, Pat, I think they are just trying to scare us off. Let's make sure the two officers who are watching our officer suspects show up. We need to find out what they know about the doings of their charges. I want them to account for the movements, if any, of those two."

Pat and Zuma got to the mall as the early morning workers were picking up their coffee, buns, and sandwiches. A few stopped to stare at the broken window and muttered things like this had never happened before on the mall. Claudia was standing in front of the stairs that took people up to her gallery. He gave her a hug and asked her if she wanted to go up and look. She nodded yes.

"Let's keep people away from the stairs. No one is to come up. If Officers LaSalle and Granger arrive, tell them to wait for me. Pat, lets take some pictures and see if we can pick up any prints from the broken bottle used."

"Joe, I'm lucky. The only damaged painting was the one in the window. None of the students were here and the insurance will pay for the repair of the window. I think I can restore the painting. Why do you think this happened? Was it vandals? Kids having stupid fun?"

"I'm not sure, Claudia dear. I think I'll be able to tell you more when I speak to the officers waiting downstairs. If you're oaky, I'd like you to go home. I'll put someone on guard who can allow the window repairman into your studio. When he's finished, if you give me your key, I will make sure the door is locked. Do you want to take the painting home with you to repair it?"

"No, Joe. Let's leave it. I'd like to show the students, when they come in, how to restore a painting. It's a complex process and there is a great history behind this kind of work. Those who do it well earn a very good living and travel to places all over the world where old paintings are fading or cracking and can't be moved for fear that it would increase the damage. In fact, there is a great mystery writer, Daniel Silva, and I read most of his books before I met you. His main character is Gabriel Allon who is a brilliant spy but acts like a detective just like you, Joe. Allon is a restorer of old masterpieces. He has to travel to all parts of the world like Vienna, London, and Rome to restore these paintings, which are extremely valuable and often considered national treasures. The paintings are difficult challenges because the pigments are mixed and old. Some of the original pigments have been lost forever. He has highly specialized equipment that he works with. I learned a lot about art restoration from reading his mysteries, and I have read over a dozen of them. I think there are now eighteen and the nineteenth is going to come out shortly. It's called *The New Girl* and involves a beautiful woman who is kidnapped. I have it on order. I think you would enjoy reading his mysteries."

"Thank you, Claudia, I think I will stay with my real-life mysteries instead of any fictionalized version. Anyone who writes about a detective over eighteen times has got to be either nuts or compulsive. The beautiful woman could be you because you are still my new girl. But I would never let you be kidnapped."

"If you change your mind, let me know. I have some of the books at home. Now, I would like to go home. This has shaken me up. Please come home early. I want to know what you may have found out."

Despite his assurances to Claudia, Joe was fearful. He was fearful at how furious he felt. This was an invasion of his private life. The fury would not only make him blind about seeing his targets and the fear would lead him to drinking the way he had when he lost his first wife. He knew that he had better speak to someone soon before he started the downward spiral and so he called Dr. Milgram. Milgram had worked with him on several cases, and Joe had a deep respect for his abilities and ethics. Milgram indicated that it would violate their future working relationship if Joe were to be a client but recommended someone whom he had the utmost confidence in, a Dr. Toby Salk. Joe called immediately and an appointment was set the same day by Salk's receptionist.

CHAPTER 15

Zuma was surprised to see that a woman opened the door to the waiting room.

"Good evening, Mr. Zuma, I'm Dr. Salk."

Her smile was reassuring, Zuma estimated her to be in her fifties, with greying hair that was clearly something she was not trying to hide. Her pantsuit was dark blue, and she measured a little over five feet tall. Her smile upon seeing him was reassuring. When they sat down in her office, she began immediately.

"My colleague, Dr. Milgram, called with your name and indicated it was urgent. How might I help you?"

He liked that she did feel the need to exchange pleasantries and seemed confident.

"About ten years ago, I lost my wife. She was killed by a hit-and-run driver. I acted really crazy and tried to track down all drivers who had bad records, and on top of that, I began drinking. I nearly lost my job. I got into a twelve-step program and did get control of my drinking. I can now drink socially. I have never had a blackout or anything approaching what I had when I was acting nuts. Yesterday, my current wife had her painting gallery receive an arson effort. I am furious and enraged, and I know these feelings the are the ones I had when I lost my first wife. I am afraid I may do something stupid and crazy or both. I don't want to do anything that would risk my marriage or my job, I am deeply satisfied with my life as it is. My marriage is a source of comfort, support, and inspiration. We have been married over three years."

"I'm impressed that you are aware of the potential dangers to you personally and professionally. Let me ask you a couple of questions, please. Have you had anything to drink since you heard about the arson? Have you discussed any of your feelings with anyone?"

"No to both of those."

"Is there a reason that you haven't mentioned your reaction to your wife?"

"I don't want to scare her."

"But, if you indicate as you have, that your wife is supportive and comforting, perhaps that should be something you would consider?"

"I would consider it, Dr. Salk, but I want to first sort it out with you so I can be clearer with myself."

"Okay. Let's go back and tell me all you can about those feelings you had when your first wife was killed."

Joe slumped down in his chair and looked down. He began talking about the daily feelings of depression and the nights of endless driving and knocking on doors, asking to see the person whom he knew lived there and had a poor driving record. He talked about his feelings of exhaustion and a beginning to despair about never finding the driver. He described how his colleagues at work were avoiding him and feeling that no one understood what it as to lose someone you loved very much. He spoke how he was short with his colleagues who suddenly seemed insensitive and uncaring. He became quiet for about fifteen seconds and began to sob. Dr. Salk waited. He was not sure how long he had sobbed. When he stopped, he inhaled deeply and looked up into Dr. Salk's eyes. He closed his eyes and became unaware of time.

"Wow, I guess I had some stuff left over."

"Yes, you did, and I think that might be influencing your reaction to the current danger you sense. Can you see the differences?"

"Yes, almost too many. No one is dead, I have a good idea who the arsonists might be, and I can have them watched carefully. The suspects have to be worried about doing anything to a police officer's family, and I think it must have been a warning and only that. No one has been physically harmed."

"Yes, and one more thing, Detective Zuma."

"What is that?"

"You have someone to talk with now."

Zuma smiled and took a very deep breath.

"Thank you, Dr. Salk. Can I pay you now?"

"Of course, whatever is best for you. Good luck and feel free to call if you need to."

"I will, but I think I will be okay."

On the way out, Zuma began humming the music to Beetles "Let It Be." He was singing the words of hope and wisdom from the song and that he heard from Dr. Salk as he dialed Claudia's number.

"Darling, I just got a shot of the Salk vaccine."

"What are you talking about Joe? Is this a joke? There is no more polio, silly. We got rid of that illness years ago."

"I got the shot anyway. It will prevent damage. I'll explain when I take you out to dine tonight. I need to talk with you."

CHAPTER 16

"Each of you were assigned to watch a possible suspect and were under strict instructions. So, what can you tell us?"

"Neither of us knew what the other was doing but each suspect drove to the mall. I saw the two officers Bailey and Robertson meet and we watched together as they went to dinner about 9:00 PM, a movie at 11:00, and a bar around 1:00 AM. One of them had parked in the parking structure and the other one on 3rd Street. They both left the bar and headed towards the parking lot. We thought that strange, but we figured that one of them was too buzzed to drive."

"Why had they been in the bar long? Had you seen them drinking?"

"No, but Detective Bailey was not walking too straight."

"That's one of the oldest cons around. Every rookie learns he can't trust a wobbly suspect. All wobblies are potential dangerous, especially if they're faking it. And if they're not faking and high, they are also dangerous as their judgments are off."

"They go into the parking lot. We wait till they get into an elevator. We see it goes to level five. We figure there coming down in one car, so I run to get my motorcycle and get ready to follow. The car doesn't come down. We wait and after ten minutes we realize they must have left the building through the backstairs."

"Another thing we teach all rookies. You never enter any building before you have secured all possible exits. I'm beginning to think you both need to go back for rookie training. Leaving an escape exit is tantamount to guaranteeing an escape."

"The next thing we hear are a few screams. The pane was broken, and the few folks who were there said the guy who did it jumped into a waiting car."

"Did you pursue the car?"

"We did but lost him. We then realized they had left their two cars back in the lot and on the street. So we staked them out. They showed up at six in the morning and we asked them where they had been and said it was personal. I told them that you would probably be talking with them and they said 'fine' but they had to get to work."

"Pat, call Thompson and tell him we need to speak with Bailey and Robertson. I can either put a report in your files about this poor behavior or you can volunteer for a repeat of the rookie training we give."

"Thank you, Detective Zuma. I think we would be better off if we go back and take those classes."

"Boss, Thompson called and said that both officers had called in sick."

"We better provide the names to all the major airports. We want to know if any flights are being booked. I would assume they are not going to leave the country, so let's do all the domestic airlines. My guess it's not to the major airport in West Virginia, Charleston, but to a nearby major airport. Also, there are a whole bunch of smaller ones in West Virginia also. So, we need to assign two new officers to do the airport search and calls and two more to watch their homes. They may just be lying low."

CHAPTER 17

The call came directly from Thompson.

"Detective Zuma, Bailey and Robertson were picked up along with the Bourne woman. She had stopped by their places and picked up each of them. It looks like the two males had made plane reservations to Memphis."

"Thompson. Hold them. Pat and I will be there within twenty minutes."

When Zuma arrived, Irving Silverberg was already there advising his clients that they did not have to answer any questions.

"You can certainly take the advice of your lawyer, but we would all look favorably upon your cooperation."

Bailey spoke. "Look, Detective, I know we are both in trouble. We will probably both lose our jobs for…"

Silverberg interrupted. "Mr. Bailey please do not talk about anything you did."

Bailey looked at Robertson. "I think my buddy is right. We are going to lose our jobs and our retirement."

"And if we find that you are linked to any of the murdered victims, you will be going to jail."

"That's enough. Detective, take my two clients and book them. I will go with them to see what your specific charges are and will wait to hear what the bail will be."

Alice Bourne who had been quiet throughout the entire conversation, asked, "Do you want me to accompany my friends down to the station? Are you going to charge me with something also?"

"Yes, we are. You have been hanging around with a major suspect in a murder case and may have been an accessory. And as you have probably figured out Ms. Bourne, from our little sing-a- long, I think you might be more than an accessory."

"Zuma, while I'm heading down for a booking, I can sing the words to that great Johnny Cash song about murder. Maybe you know it. I'm sure you know him since you know a lot of our southern singers. It's called, 'I Hung My Head.' I'll just say the words and edit it for your benefit.

> *"My brother's rifle*
> *Went off in my hand*
> *The sheriff he asked me*
> *Why had I run*
> *And then it come to me*
> *Just what I had done*
> *And all for no reason*
> *Just one piece of lead*
> *I hung my head*
>
> *Explain to the court room*
> *What went through your mind*
> *And we'll ask the jury*
> *What verdict they find*
> *I hung my head*
> *I prayed for God's mercy*
> *'Cause soon I'd be dead.*
> *I hung my head*
> *I hung my head*

"So maybe, Detective, I will hang my head but maybe not. You never can tell what is going to happen with a jury. There's got to be a lot of sympathy for a poor coal miner's daughter. And I'm sure my southern accent and charm, my great legs, and good looks won't hurt me with a northern jury. I hope there are lots of men sitting in the box."

"We will see, Ms. Bourne. But now I need to cuff you. I know you feel that there is no need to do this to the three of you, but we are going to follow official procedure. So just get in the car with my assistant and me."

During the booking, Pat, who was off to the side spoke to Zuma. "I noticed something, boss, when I was cuffing the three of them."

"What was that?"

"On the inside of each of their left-hand wrists was the number seven. I thought at first it could be a question mark but was pretty sure it was the number seven because I saw it on each of their wrists. What do you make of that, boss?"

The toothpick came out and the humming started.

"Seven is the he same number of miners who went over to the company and sided against the striking miners."

After the booking, the three suspects were told that they would be under house arrest until their bail was posted. The bail fee came in two days later as Zuma had argued that all three were flight risks. The fee for each was $50,000. Irving Silverberg showed up with $150,000 in cash.

"Would Silverberg be willing to lose that money, boss? They could fly the coop and disappear in those hills and we could never find them. Once folks knew we were hunting for them, they would all clam up."

"I'm sure it's not his money. They must be pooling resources. We have got to keep tabs on them. They may end up driving and not flying. Let's keep the airport alert in place. There is a court date in two weeks. Let's get to the other names on the list. Maybe they can give us some ideas about how this gang raises or gets its money. Let's stop calling them the West Virginia Gang. The WV gang will be an easier way to talk about them. I need to checki with Claudia."

"Joe, what did you find out about the arson?"

"We are pretty sure we know who did it. We're going to book them. But it was not an attempt to hurt anyone. They wanted to scare me."

"Is this related to the case you are working on?"

"Yes, I know they must believe I'm getting closer. They would never want to kill me as that would mean the chair or life imprisonment, so their best hope is to frighten me. They thought it would be easier to create a fear by attacking you. It would have been too risky for them to just go after me. What would your famous detective Allon do in a case like this? Any thoughts?"

"I'm sure if the two of you were working on this case, you would be thinking exactly alike."

"Thank you, Claudia, and now let's go to dinner so I can be alone with my old girl."

"Joe, I know you're going to end up reading that book. I'm sure, no I'm positive you will love it."

"Maybe you're right, but I don't need a new girl. I'm very happy with my old girl."

———∽∽———

At the office, Pat and Zuma were working on board. There were five victims and six suspects.

"Every one of the victims except Slater and his son Saul and the woman lying next to Slater could be targets for a revenge killing, Pat. And even Slater could be a target for revenge, but his murder would be unrelated to the strike. Pat, we have the trial for Bailey and Robertson coming up in three days, and I want to make sure we have tabs on those miners who sided with the mine company. We need surveillance at their home and to follow any of them if they leave. We should have at least two people to start with, and it needs to be for twenty-four hours. I'd like you and I to do the interviewing. We can divvy it up. Let's start today. It might help us in the trial that's coming up. We can talk at the end of the day. They should be home as they are likely to be retired."

CHAPTER 18

"Welcome, Detective. Sit down and take a load off. Can I get you a drink of water or something else that can refresh you?"

"No, thank you. As I said on the phone, we have some questions about your living in West Virginia, the strike, and your coming north."

"Yes, I got your call, and I'm happy to talk with you. When we left our hometown, Detective Zuma, it was because we were being yelled at, called names, and cursed by most of the other townspeople. At best, we got cold shoulders. It was hard for us to leave but we had to. My family had lived in the town for four generations. It was leaving a way of life that was all we knew. My wife had no one who would talk to her. When she would walk into a store, people would walk out. Even the clerks made her wait and wait. When we came here to California we bonded together. It was a strange climate, no real seasons, and we weren't used to your traffic, your pace, and the prices. Everyone focused on our accents, either they thought they were cute or strange. We thought the same of you. We felt like we were in a foreign country."

"Did you ever discuss the idea that someone from your town might be seeking revenge for you siding with the Van Elms Mining Company?"

"We talked about it. When one of us, Dan Albert, was shot about three years ago in a drive-by we kind of dismissed it as something that happened in this foreign country of yours. We don't have drive-bys in our town."

"What happened when the second person was shot?"

"That was a year later. It was Mark Bittman. He got killed in a carjacking that was accompanied by a shooting and resulted in his death. Seemed like a planned murder to me. We began to argue. Some felt that this was still a coincidence, again saying that carjackings just don't happen in our town. No one would want to steal any of the cars that we drove. They were all old, beat up, and all close to dying. But even though we argued, we agreed we needed to be more careful. We all got security cameras and alarms and made sure we each had all the phone numbers from the five of us who were left."

"Thank you. You have been very helpful, Mr. Cooper. I regret to inform you that there are now only three of you left. Mr. Roman and Mr. Haskin were each found in what looks like to be a carefully planned murder."

"I'll have to let the others know as soon as you leave, Detective. Sorry to hear that. That's quite a shock. And two of us murdered so very close together. They were good people. I wonder if they are getting desperate. I guess you're right, there are only three of us left."

"Perhaps they are planning more shortly, Mr. Cooper. I have one more question, actually two more, that either of you could address. Do you have any idea who the people are that might be seeking revenge? You mentioned 'they' when you thought they might be getting desperate. Who are 'they'?"

"I think that's an easy one. Anyone who was on the other side of the picket line that we were on. Everyone in town who was supporting the strike was angry at us. I'm very sure that no one in town was neutral, I would also imagine that if any of them came north because Van Elms did shut down, they would be the most likely candidates for getting back at us. Revenge runs deep in our culture, but the ones who came north would have more opportunity to seek it."

"And my last question is how you imagine, if there is a gang of revenge seekers would be able to raise money for helping each other? None of them has struck it rich. Where do you think they might be getting money from? Do you think they are selling or running drugs?"

"That's another easy one, Detective. I'm sure they have nothing to do with drugs. In West Virginia, we always saw that as a northern thing. We just liked our moonshine. No, I think the money comes from an old strong tradition. From where we all come from, we learn to help each other out. That's something we do and teach our children to do. That's one of the reasons that the company had such difficulty in breaking the strike and had to bring in outsiders. The striking miners were helping each other in whatever ways they could, and even the few townspeople who were not connected to the mine would also help. As I said no one was neutral. Van Elms had to bring in outsiders to break the strike. I assume the folks who are out to get us pool their resources whenever necessary."

"Thank you again. Please be cautious. We have posted some officers outside your home to give you twenty-four-hour protection. Here is my card, and if you see anything suspicious don't hesitate to call."

"That's mighty kind of you, Detective Zuma. It feels like good old southern hospitality. If my friends or I hear of anything, we will call you. Are you sure you wouldn't like a drink before you get on the road in your northern, crazy-making traffic?"

Zuma laughed out loud. "No, thank you, I'm used to the traffic. Speaking of traffic, you might want to try something different. I can suggest a road that you might enjoy. It's a highway that's celebrated in song and it's called Ventura Highway. The lyrics say, 'the days are longer, and the nights are stronger than moonshine.'"

"That makes sense about days being longer, but I sincerely doubt, Detective Zuma, whether anything can be found that is stronger than the moonshine we make back home."

Zuma laughed again and smiled on his way to the car. He was deeply impressed how, despite being pursued by people who wanted to kill him that this southern gentleman could be gracious and crack a joke. He knew he would tell Claudia about it, but he thought that it was a way of life that he wished would exist up here in the north. He knew a song that mentioned northern and southern hospitality and wondered if Bourne would know it. He knew the version by Peggy Lee and sang the words to one of the stanzas from "I Like Men" to himself.

"I like the masculine; I like the mind.
And any other kind that I can find.
But will always Choose Southern Hospitality over Northern Pride."

The trial resulted in fines of ten thousand dollars, community service of five hundred hours, and a year's probation for each of the two male suspects. Alice Bourne received a less demanding sentence. Her accent and legs must have worked because she was fined a symbolic dollar and required to volunteer at a shelter for battered women. The two officers were immediately suspended and knew they would not be allowed to return to police work. On the way out of the courtroom after hearing the sentences imposed by the jury and backed by the judge, Alice Bourne cornered Zuma and said, "That was a small price to pay, Detective. Revenge often has a good payoff. I told you, Detective, Southern charm always wins over Northern lust."

Zuma was not disappointed in the outcomes. The district attorney would not seek the kind of penalties that Zuma and Vasquez had argued for. He kept indicating that the evidence was at best circumstantial; there were no witnesses and no gun. There was motive but that was not enough. He was hoping that revenge would still be operative and that he would be prepared. He didn't have to wait long.

A morning newscast two days after the trial was over reported that a recently convicted police officer was shot outside a home. The detective, a Mr. Bailey, knocked on the door and was greeted by the homeowner with a gun. Upon seeing that the officer had a pistol in his hand, the homeowner fired at the officer, killing him instantly. The newscaster indicated that at this time there were no further details to report as the homeowner was being questioned by the police. Zuma, upon arriving at work, went immediately to the interrogation room. He was greeted by a familiar sounding voice, and accent and the warmth that he had labeled as southern hospitality.

"Why, Detective Zuma, right nice to see you again. I was hoping you would be coming in so I wouldn't be kept here too long. I know you would be able to explain why I was prepared and answered the door with a gun."

"Have they offered you a drink, Mr. Cooper?"

"They offered me one, Detective, but I turned it down. I didn't feel they wanted to satisfy my thirst but were just following some official procedure. I know if you get me a drink it is because you care if I need one or would like one."

Zuma again admired this man. He was in control and still had a sense of humor and pride even though he was sitting in a detention room.

"I'm going to order you a drink and then I would like you to tell me what happened this morning. Take your time and try to remember everything you can."

"Now that's what I consider a friendly invitation, Detective. I shall be happy to talk."

Mr. Cooper spoke slowly and went through all the details of what time the knock came, how he was expecting trouble and had gone to the door with his gun in his hand, and upon opening it, seeing the office with a pistol in his hand, he fired his weapon.

"I knew it was either him or me. I guess I'm lucky."

"I see no further need to detain you, Mr. Cooper. Thanks for coming in, and I'll have someone give you a ride back to your home."

"Thank you, Detective, for a most pleasant chat and your considerate offer to have someone drive me home. My wife will be glad to see me, and I will tell her about your graciousness."

"Yes, please say hello to her, and I'm sure you will still be keeping all your alarms on. I don't think the revenge vendetta is quite over. Were still going to keep a guard close by. I need to figure out where our detective was."

"I agree, Detective. I will continue to be cautious and safe."

Pat and Zuma checked with the other detective who reported that the knock on the door looked as if it was a newspaper delivery. The car had "Orange County Register" painted on both sides.

Zuma groaned. Why would someone who lived in Playa del Rey want an Orange County newspaper. He realized the detective doesn't read newspapers and, therefore, wouldn't know the names of any newspapers or where they came from unless the city was in the title.

"Pat, get this guy out of here and show him all the names of all the newspapers that are printed in a hundred-mile radius. Officer Lyons, I will be testing you later. I expect you to give the names of at least twenty newspapers. Pat, please run a check on the car left on Mr. Cooper's street. Any car that is sold has to be reported to the DMV. Maybe the seller has sold other cars. Let's see if the dealer has sold other cars to any of our suspects. Can you do that right now? I'll wait while you call."

"Boss, the buyer of the car used in the shooting turned up a big surprise. It was our young ingénue, Christina Marshall. And the dealer said he had sold her two other cars. She always paid in cash. She asked him to not report the sales to the DMV. He said he wouldn't, but he did."

"Remember what I said, Pat? There has got to be someone who is organizing these hits, someone who call the shots with timing and has resources."

"Should we bring her in, boss?'

"Not yet. Let's put a tail on her and make sure she and her daddy are followed. Maybe she will be visiting some of the other members of the gang, members who we don't even know about. I think we need to go back and finish the training."

CHAPTER 19

"Gentlemen and ladies, all of the trainings we do are very different. Yours has not only been different, it has touched on issues that go beyond racism or sexism. It is about your basic role as police officers, which I mentioned to you is your major responsibility which is to protect and serve. Our training has uncovered some who did not protect and certainly did not serve. You are to be given credit for that. On this last day I would like to see if we can tie up any loose ends. Questions for each other or for me? Feelings you would like to express? Suggestions you have for Chief Thompson or for me?"

"I, for one, have had trouble thinking about the training that we have had. A couple of bad apples has upset me. And the thought that there may be a larger group involved in murders is very disturbing. I have nothing against the training, I suppose it's good that we found out who was unreliable."

"But since we didn't know, the training helped uncover things it shows me that you can't trust anyone. So, the training has not been helpful to me. It has just made me more wary."

Murmurs of agreement. Zuma spoke.

"If the training has trained or helped you to be more cautious, I would feel it has been successful. Before the training, you felt and believed you could usually or even only trust someone if they were of a similar race or gender. Now, you know that you need to know much more about a person. Similarity should not automatically mean trustworthiness and difference should not automatically mean untrustworthy. That is why we suggest talking with those who don't look and speak like us and those who do look or speak like us. That is why we suggest getting to know someone's personal life. I recognized that each of us have a different sense of what is private and what isn't, but the more we do know about the other the less likely we are going to be sabotaged or involved in actions as police officers that undermine the department mission. Cross-race friendships in this department are more likely to mean cross-race acceptance of the communities you serve. That sound simple but it's deep because genuine cross-race friendships rarely occur. You have shown that you are ready to do that. Do I know if this training will bring about the results that we hoped to attain when we first met? No, I don't. Do I know if there will now be less lawsuits or less shootings? I honestly don't know. But time will tell. And I know that the principles of our training have proven themselves to be of value in many other situations. If it works here, your precinct will become a flagship for the country and its future with police community relations. Pat, can you read the reminders we want to conclude with?"

"Sure, boss. First, a citizen can refuse to answer any questions you ask. Second, you can only pat down someone if you think there is a concealed weapon. Third, they can refuse any further search. Fourth, if you decide to arrest someone, you have to indicate why you are doing it. Are there any questions or comments? No?"

"I have one for you, Detective Zuma. It's a bit personal. Don't you feel that as part of your effort to know the other better as well as know your own that you should learn to speak Spanish?"

"I'm glad you asked. I have learned from doing this work with you that I have avoided doing that. I see that as one of my failings. I plan to rectify that in the immediate future. I'm going to have Detective Vasquez talk to me in Spanish as much as possible. And I am going to take a class in speaking Spanish."

An officer yells. "Detective Zuma, I will invite you to our home for a dinner with my six children and you'll get earfuls of Spanish."

Everyone laughed.

"I'd like that but give me a couple of months, so I don't just spend the whole evening being embarrassed because I keep asking for translations." Everybody laughed again. "So, again, Detective

Vasquez and I thank you. Chief Thompson, would you like to add a word?"

"I'd like for each of us to come up with suggestions on how to further this goal that Detective Zuma mentioned. How do we deepen our relationships with one another? You can hand them in to our suggestion box. They can have your names or be anonymous. I want to personally thank you both. I am glad I found you and that you were able to do this work for us. Okay, folks, let's go do the thing we are paid for, protecting and serving. And now when you think of the phrase or see it on our cars or hear it from politicians, it will personally mean to you that you are protecting all and serving all."

"Boss, I'm impressed with you and the officers. I think the training worked."

"You may be right. Time will tell, but right now I feel good about what we did and what they seem ready to do."

"Yo tambien."

"Gracias por todo, Pat."

"Jefe, vamos a trabajar."

"Who do you think we should start with?"

"Empecemos con Cynthia Marshall, Mr. Marshall, and Alice Bourne."

"Two of those are major suspects. I think it will take some time before we track Bourne down. But we can go to the Marshall's home right now."

———ɯ———

"Mr. Marshall, in an article written after the strike was broken, a researcher found the names of seven of the people who had refused to go on strike. Apparently, their lives were made difficult by those who had walked the picket line and they all had to leave."

"Yeah, while we were striking and starving because we couldn't buy food in the company store, they were living off the fat of the company and even getting free food at the store. The damn company also started enforcing hunting laws so we couldn't hunt for food. We suffered, they didn't. Seemed only right they should suffer later."

"I'm sure you and others felt that way. Do you know of any efforts on the part of the strikers to get back at the seven who did not strike?"

"Wouldn't surprise me a bit. We don't like it if someone sells out his fellow workers. I'm sure people didn't forget. I hope their lives were miserable after they left."

"Mr. Marshall, I don't know how miserable some of their lives were, but I do know that four of the strikers are dead. We have good reason to believe that all four were murdered. Do you know anything about who might have been involved in those murders?"

"Detective, I assume you are here because you believe I had something to do with those murders. If I did, I certainly would not be telling you anything. Growing up in a mining town, all of us had enough trouble with snitches to hate them. I ain't going to be a snitch. And neither will my wife."

"So, you're saying you do know something but won't talk to me?"

"I don't think I said that at all. What I said and I'm repeating it is that I ain't no goddamn snitch."

"Mr. and Mrs. Marshall, we can bring you in as suspects and make your lives uncomfortable with a trial and some jail time."

"Discomforts will not be new to us. For us it's a way of life. Our daughter has money now, and I'm sure she'll get us a good lawyer."

"I'm sure she will. We will be in touch. Thank you for your time today."

"Pat, what did you think?"

"Whatever he says about not knowing, I just don't believe him. Those strikers are a very tight bunch. He may be the oldest but I'm sure he was one of the leaders. If I had to guess, I think he would still be a leader. In English, we spell it with 'ea' but in Spanish it's with an 'li.' No matter how you spell it, I think he is running the show."

"I agree, Pat, or if he isn't, he's behind who is. We're going to have to watch him like a hawk."

"You know, boss, he is very smart. He's not going to do anything that would lead us to anyone who is involved in these murders. Maybe a better way to get to him is through the daughter, la hija. Let's go visit now."

—m—

"Ms. Marshall, I'm sure your dad called ahead and told you what kind of information we are hoping to obtain from you. I am even surer that you will indicate that you have no knowledge of who the leader is and how this team of West Virginia brothers might be operating."

"You're right, Detective. I can't and wouldn't if I could. We learn early about not snitching early on in West Virginia, and it was a big thing my daddy taught me."

"Like father, like daughter."

"You're right again, Detective, and I'm proud of it."

"Speaking of being proud, Ms. Marshall, how is your career going?"

"Happy to talk about that with you. I'm producing a play that I think most Northerners would recognize and even appreciate."

"Tell me more, please."

"Sure, right now I'm debating with the writer. I would like the title of the play to be "You Load 16 Tons and What Do You Get?"

The author would like "I Owe my Soul to the Company Store." The play is an enactment of the strike that my daddy and the others were involved with."

"Does the play talk about what happens to the people who sided with the mining company and had to leave town and came north as well as some of their murders?"

"Absolutely. We want the audience to walk out with a sense that it could be the revenge that is part of our Southern culture and a sense that these were clever Southern boys."

"Does the play make it clear or even hint at who the leader is among your clever Southern boys?"

"You're probably going to have to see the play to see if there is any hint along those lines, Detective."

"How do I see it? When will that be?"

"Were practicing and right now just reading to each other. We don't have sets yet and haven't figured out how much music we need."

"How did you get actors to play southerners? Did you do the casting?"

"I advertised and interviewed."

"Where are you doing the reading?"

"It's a tiny theatre in North Hollywood. I can give you the name, but I will not allow you to come in and hear any aspects of the work."

"And who is your writer?"

"It is one of my closest friends. This is a piece that is very close to her heart."

"My turn to guess, Ms. Marshall. It must be Alice Bourne."

"You are correct, Detective Zuma. If there are no more questions about the play or my dad or the crimes, I'd like to get back to my work."

"You said you were the producer. Have you wanted to act in the play? It would not hurt your career to be both the producer and an actor in the work by your friend."

"I have thought about it. I'm thinking of playing the wife of one of the strike breakers. It would be a stretch for me to play a scab. I'd have to work hard to get into that role, but I think it would be good experience and could boost my career."

Zuma was impressed with the confidence that this relatively unknown actor and first-time producer showed in the interview. He wondered if the source of confidence could be something else other than the play.

"One more question, Ms. Slater. We found you purchased three cars but neither one is registered in California. Would you mind telling us where they are registered or located?"

"I had them delivered to my brothers in our hometown in West Virginia."

"Could you give us the address?"

"Detective, why don't you call the local police chief in Mongahlia. I'm sure he will tell you."

The toothpick came out as he left Christina Slater and the humming began.

"Okay, boss. What's blowin' in the wind?"

"I think she must be confident that whoever is doing the murders is a safe and secure secret and perhaps more confident that there will be a successful effort to get to all seven. Pat, we need to send someone down to make the trip and speak to the chief in that town. I don't think he will be cooperative, and our guy might have to do some more legwork with folks. We need to locate the brothers. That's more important than the cars."

CHAPTER 20

"Boss, I checked with the theatre. The rent has been paid for three months and its used usually about three time per week, usually in the evening after seven. They stay till around ten. There are no more than six or seven of them. It could be used after that since the guard leaves at midnight. The manager also said they are very responsible with the use of the theatre. The chairs are returned to their original spots, there are no cigarette butts on the floor, and there is nothing to indicate that they had been munching during rehearsal. If he didn't know they were renting the place and the security did not see them, it's as if they were never there."

"Did the manager say whether he was able to witness an actual rehearsal?"

"He said he had asked, but the director said that the readings were private."

"We're still going to have to watch it twenty-four-seven for any evidence of use, especially careful to be there when security is not on duty."

"Let's go back and speak to Ms. Cynthia Marshall again."

"Detectives, my lawyer told me I was under no obligation to tell you anything about the play."

"You lawyer is correct. You are under no obligation to answer our questions, Ms. Slater. But you have moved to the top of our suspect list, and I'm sure you know what that might mean for you.

We can get a warrant for all of the following: monitoring your e mails; examining your phone and we will be able to walk into your home unannounced. And of course, you will be followed every day and night."

"I'm going to get Alice to put all of that into the play. Maybe one of the acts can be called, 'North versus South' or 'Northern Cops and Southern Boys.'"

Pat jumped in. "Ms. Marshall, a better title might be, 'A losing Battle, Again.'"

"I'll tell the writer, Detective Vasquez, but I'm sure she won't like it."

"Well, if she really waits to see the end of the real-life story, she may not be able to write any ending. So, you had better get her going on writing this play."

"You know, Pat. I think she told us the truth about everything. There is a play, and I think the actors are the real-life West Virginia gang. And they do meet and show up. They don't have to all be there meet physically but the only one who could be the organizer and leader is Christina or her father."

"Boss, I still think the Bourne gal might be the top gun here. I think we have to see if any of our suspects, the minor ones and the two you mentioned, have any kind of contact with her."

"You're right, Pat. We've got sixteen tons of stuff to do."

"More stuff, boss. Waiting outside. She's an old suspect waiting to see you. Should I let her rent in?"

Zuma's ears perked up. It was certainly strange that any suspect would show up at the precinct but stranger that an old suspect would be wanting to see him.

"Let her in, Pat." Zuma was going through his mind thinking of whom it might be when the door opened and he saw Sonia Tabachnick.

"Detective Zuma, I've come here to tell you that your suspicions were correct. I did kill my husband. I suspect your wife talked you out of pursuing me. Going to court would have been a terrible embarrassment to my daughter. She would have been ridiculed in school and would be the brunt of terrible names. I want to confess now because I believe she would be better off in hearing it from me rather than reading about it in a newspaper or seeing it on TV. I want her to know it from me rather than from any other source. So, I'm ready for whatever you think I should do. I can sign a confession, which might be the easiest thing."

Zuma was taken aback. He knew that Sonia had been doing lots of good things in the community. Claudia had told him she was conducting a furniture-building class for seniors at SafePaths and was also volunteering at a home for battered women. He was reminded of how Claudia had argued for his using mercy in his judgment of Sonia and allow the mercy to be a factor in his not hauling her off to jail.

"Sonia, I'm not sure whether I can or should accept your confession. In fact, a court might find it outrageous and not believe you after all the years have passed. But I, myself, would have a problem now, even with a confession, because there is s no evidence of a victim. I don't think the court would see your confession as anything but bizarre and might even see you as bit nuts. I think the only way you could end up serving a sentence is if you were to provide some evidence of an actual victim. That would be your husband. Can you do that?"

"That would be pretty impossible, Detective. As you probably figured out, I put his body in one of my large pieces and shipped it off to India. I heard they put it in one of their museums that stressed contemporary works. Eventually, I'm sure the smells would have required they open up the drawers and when they did that, there would not be much left for them to use to identify anything. Whatever remains were left, I'm sure, by now they have cremated."

"Mrs. Tabachnick, you're giving my comments more credibility. There is no body or any evidence of a victim. This would make it very difficult for a jury to convict you. And even with a confession, a jury would probably find you not guilty and a bit off your rocker. That judgment might be as difficult for your daughter to handle as the one about murder."

"I know I'm repeating myself, Detective, but I think it's best my daughter finds out from me rather than any other source. Do you have any suggestions as to what I might do?"

"Mrs. Sonia Tabachnick, perhaps I can give you a piece of wisdom that I've acquired since I'm a bit older than you. Sometimes, it's okay to keep secrets and even to go to your grave with them. If revealing your truth is going to hurt and hurt badly, what do you have to gain? I think, in this case, the only gain would be to relieve your conscience. That is not enough, in my opinion, for you to hurt your daughter. You've done a lot of good, and I'm sure you will continue to do well. I also believe that my wife would not be a happy camper if I decided at this point to drop the value of mercy that she helped me understand. She would lose respect for me if I neglected to use what she worked so hard for me to understand."

"Thank you, Detective. You have been most helpful to me. I would like to express my gratefulness to you with something more than words. I would like to give you some furniture that I have designed. I have two lovely chairs that I think you and your wife would enjoy."

"I am not allowed to accept gifts, but I'm sure some of the people that you know would be happy to receive whatever you have made. Thank you for coming in. I assume I will see you at some of the SafePath functions. When I see you there with you daughter, I'm sure I will feel that I've done a good deed."

"Blessings on you, Detective. I look forward to seeing you and your lovely wife at all the functions."

"Claudia, I had a visit today from the person you convinced me not to prosecute. She wanted to confess, and I convinced her that it was senseless as there was no evidence of a victim and, at this point, confessing would hurt her daughter and that some secrets can go to the grave with you."

"Joe, you did good again. I do want you to know that I have no secrets that I'm planning to go to the grave with."

Neither do I, darling. Except I have a secret that I want to tell you." Zuma started humming and singing the words to a song that he knew from the Beatles. "Listen, do you want to know a secret? I'm in love with you, ooh…"

Claudia joined in as they looked into each other's eyes and sang, "I'm in love with you, ooh."

As they were singing to each other on the phone, Pat knocked and entered.

"Boss, we got another suspect. This is not an old one, and I don't think this one's going to confess. Should I let her in?"

Alice Bourne strode confidently into Zuma's office and without being invited, took a seat facing him.

"Well, this is quite a surprise. I can't imagine why you dropped in to speak to us, Ms. Bourne. I'm sure you're not here to confess to any murders."

Alice laughed. "Why would I do that detective I'm a writer, not a murderer."

"Those aren't necessarily mutually exclusive, Ms. Bourne."

"No, they aren't, but in my case they are. I'm here to ask you to stop harassing me from working on this play. It could be a big one but right now, your team of Sherlock Holmes losers are following me everywhere I go and it's hard for me to focus on the writing when I realize they're outside my door or down the street."

"Well, I realize this must be an inconvenience for you, but you must realize why you're a prime suspect in at a number of murders."

"I'm not sure I want to hear this, but I'll indulge you, Detective."

"There is a lot of indirect evidence. Number one, is that you hang out with a number of people who we are convinced have been involved with murders. Number two, you were and are close to these people in terms of background, and so you may know things about them and they may know things about you that they are keeping secretive. So, we watch you to see whom you are talking with or spending more time with. We are hoping that someone in the gang will feel an obligation to confess. I believe any confession will involve you so you will move from being a suspect to being on trial. Number three, you had a lot to gain from the death of Slater. Since you and Christina are best buds, she would have money now from insurance to help you write and direct a play, which would take you into the limelight that you feel you deserve. And finally, number four, we think you're one of the smartest in your gang from West Virginia and we think that you could be calling the shots."

"Detective Zuma. That's very imaginative. But all speculative. It probably would make a very good play. Have you thought about writing as a second career?"

It was Zuma's turn to laugh. "Actually I have thought about it, but if I became famous, it would put me in the limelight which I do not want. I am quite happy in the work I do, solving real crimes as opposed to inventing them and solving them. It has a bit of an appeal but not enough for me to want to change my life."

"Boss, I'm sorry, but I need to interrupt. An emergency call just came in. It looks like we have another corpse."

CHAPTER 21

"Alice, I think your timing is perfect. I'm sure you wanted to be here at the same time that you knew that something was being carried out. This would make your innocence look real and would appeal to my sense of fairness and create the effect you wanted in me to stop the harassment. In fact, it has the opposite effect. It just convinces me of how clever you are. If you will excuse me now, Detective Vasquez and I have got to get to the scene of a crime. I'm sure it's related to all the others, and as I said earlier, probably to you as well."

"Detective Zuma, I would like to make you an offer. If you could stop harassing me and let me finish my play, I will provide you with information regarding the murders. Zuma stared at Alice with disbelief. He did not believe that the loyalty between people from West Virginia would be broken by anyone, especially not by someone as strong as Alice.

"I have no doubt that we will eventually find out what we need to know about the murders, so I don't see what I have to gain by agreeing to stop my careful monitoring of you. You gain peace of mind to write, I don't see what my gain is."

"You gain a guarantee that I will give you information and you will gain a certain speed to the solution to the murders which I'm sure you would like to expedite as quickly as possible. This means a lot to me. It is an important play and it will bring to attention the plight of minors throughout the country which still continues to this day. Detective Zuma, do you realize that sixty to seventy miners still die each year in the US coal mining industry? Few states escape disaster with my southern states of West Virginia and Kentucky being hardest hit.

"Here are the names of the towns and states and the number of miners killed in some of the major explosions in our country. I plan to have them flashing on a screen in my play. For your benefit, Detective, I will repeat them. I know them by heart. The first one that I mention occurred in 1907, and it was and is the biggest mining disasters of this century. And of course, it happened in the state we were raised in. Everyone in our town knew that date and the number of miners killed. It is something we were taught, and we all grew up knowing about. It was a dark shadow adding to the fumes and coal dust we were breathing. The date was December 6 and it made Christmas a little harder to celebrate. And once Pearl Harbor happened on the 7th, it made the shadow even darker. The town is the first one to flash on the screen. I will recite names of the towns and states and the number killed. I plan to recite at least ten names although I could do sixteen. Here they are, Detective. You will note that five of the sixteen occurred in West Virginia.

362, Monongah, West Virginia
259, Cherry, Illinois
263, Dawson, New Mexico
91, Bartley, West Virginia
72, St. Clairsville, Ohio
111, Centralia, Illinois
119, West Frankfort, Illinois
78, Farmington, West Virginia
38, Hyden, Kentucky
91, Kellogg, Idaho
15, Redstone, Colorado
27, Emery County, Utah
13, Brookwood, Alabama
12, Tallmansville, West Virginia
6, Huntington, Utah, and
29, Naoma, West Virginia.

"I have left out a number of other states. Mining kills and injures more people than any other work in the world.

"And I'm not even mentioning what black lung disease did to so many miners. And I'm not mentioning the families that lived near the mine and developed all kinds of other ailments from breathing in the dust. That's why I think my play is important. Mine owners still don't value lives over profits.

Zuma wavered. "When do you think you can finish writing your play?"

"I think I could finish it up in two weeks. We would need three weeks maybe four to produce it. We have to find a venue. I want to big one. I would say within two months you'll have the information you want."

"I'll agree, Alice, provided you put on that ankle brace, so we know where you are and you don't leave town or the country. I will put someone outside your residence to make sure you're not hanging out with the others and that you go to the theater to work on the production after you finish the writing, which I know you can do at home. If you can agree to that we have a deal."

"Thank you, Detective Zuma."

"What do you think, Pat?"

"I agree with her, boss. We have nothing to lose, we can always follow her. If we become suspicious of what she is doing, we can pick her up. I would like to believe that when the time is up, she will deliver something and that will be the truth. I think she is a straight shooter. No pun intended. That play of sure sounds like it could be a powerful one."

"Yeah, Pat. She is ten feet tall."

"Those people from West Virgina seem to be all over our town, boss. Nothing has happenned that is not conncected to them."

"So far you're right, Pat."

The body was found next to a 7-Eleven store. There was one bullet straight into the heart. It had been fired from a distance and someone near the scene reported hearing the gun shot, looking up, and seeing a car speed away. The witness said it had a West Virginia license plate. There was a wallet with money and an ID. Nothing had been touched. It was not a robbery. Both Pat and Zuma believed it must have been done by the West Virginia gang, but the MO was completely different. After notifying the dead man's family and doing a background check, they found out to their surprise that the man was not from West Virginia and, according to his family, never travelled in the south. According to his wife, he had worked all his life for the department of motor vehicles. The DMV confirmed this.

"Pat, let's assume that this latest killing was designed to throw us off the trail, to start worrying about another member of the gang who wasn't in the gang but would be loyal and beholden to them. Who do we know who might still be in West Virginia who would feel that loyalty?"

"The only ones that have been mentioned are those sibling of Christina, the other Marshall children."

"Correct, Pat. We need to get moving on that trip to West Virginia that I mentioned earlier. I'm pretty sure we won't get any help from their local police as to their whereabouts or their travels. Let's just assume it was one or both of the siblings. We need to send some of our guys down there and look for any Marshall. Try and find your sharpest guys and ones that are sensitive to differences in customs. If they locate them and interview them, we might be able to figure out how to implicate them with the suspects we already have here.'

"Got it, boss. I know just the right ones."

"If they can't find them, follow up with DMV registrations in the name of Marshall. The last two years of registrations should do it."

Zuma wondered why two brothers would need three cars. You only did that so you wouldn't be easily recognized or to prevent someone from noticing a similar pattern of behavior. You would be less likely to notice patterns if cars were different. And you wouldn't want to be recognized or your patterns to be discovered if you did drugs. He started humming as he pulled out the toothpick.

Drugs had never entered into this entire investigation. Someone from the South had said, "Drugs area northern thing. We do booze in the South."

CHAPTER 22

Zuma received a call that the actors had showed up and were going into the theatre. He and Pat drove over there after telling the phone caller that if anyone left, he should be called right away. When they arrived and knocked on the door, they were greeted by Christiana Slater.

"Hi, Detectives, I assume you want to watch us rehearse, but I would ask you to please not come in. If you do, Alice and I will stop the rehearsal. We do not want you to see the play before it is ready. You will definitely be invited, and we will give you complimentary tickets."

"As you wish. But we will want the names of all of your actors."

"We want to find out where all these actors live and where they came from. We can post a few of our officers outside till their rehearsal is finished and have each actor give us their home address. This way, they will realize that the case is something we are working on."

"Detective, Mr. Silverberg taught me that they do not have to answer any questions besides their name unless you provide them a reason and the reason has to be related to your suspicions."

"She's right, boss. I'd like to be one of the interviewers. They might remember me if they were in the training. It will lend more credibility to our ongoing work."

"I agree, Pat. Good thinking."

The next few weeks passed without any suspicious behavior on the part of the actors, Christina, Alice, or the Marshalls. The actors and rehearsals were ongoing and occasionally the Marshalls would show up. After rehearsals, some would gather in a bar for a late-night bite or a couple of drinks, but Zuma's observers said that no phone calls were made during their bar time at the bar.

Opening night arrived and the complimentary tickets were sent to Zuma at the precinct. He wrote a check, not wanting to be seen as receiving payments from suspects and brought it to the theatre. When they parked near the theatre, they heard a roar coming towards them. As they entered the heard the crowd singing, but more like screaming at the top of their lungs. John Denver was barely audible.

"Almost heaven, West Virginia
Blue Ridge Mountains, Shenandoah River
Life is old there, older than the trees
Younger than the mountains, blowing like a breeze
Country roads, take me home
To the place I belong
West Virginia, mountain mamma"

The ninety-nine-seat venue was packed with an additional ten people in the standing room section at the rear. Everyone in the audience was singing away. Zuma and Pat had center seats in the second row. It took a while for Christina to quiet the audience down.

"I want to introduce you to our very own mountain momma who, with this play, is going to take every one of us back home."

Wild cheers and applause erupted.

"I'm very happy to see so many of my friends and others that I don't know but I assume are here to celebrate the state we all love. I hope that you can please spread the word to those who don't know our state. It is my hope that with this play, the world will stop seeing us as hillbillies who do nothing but drink, hunt, and intermarry. We don't need to be civilized as they tried to do in that terrible sitcom about us called the Beverly Hills Hillbillies. We are civilized, moral, and hardworking."

More cheers and applause. Some shouted, "Go tell 'em mountain mamma!" and "They could learn from us."

"It has been my pleasure in writing about you. I feel honored that I have been able to write about you, wonderful people, and our marvelous state and people. I hope I have been to capture the courage you have, the hardworking ethic you have, and the hopes you all hold for a better life for your families. I hope also that this play reminds all Americans of the immorality and injustice committed by mine owners as it draws upon one of the most famous strikes in our country's history. Mostly, I hope that you see yourselves in these heroic characters. And of course, I hope you all enjoy the show."

Everyone cheered and applaused.

During the play, the audience was very reactive. They cheered the strikers and booed at mention of the mine owners and the strike breakers. The strongest reactions came from the sexism depicted in the South and the North. To Zuma's surprise, about half the audience was comprised of women. The music was loud and when the time came in the play for the audience to see the names of the coal mine disasters on the screen, there was a sudden hush. As the last name of the town, state, and number killed was recited by Alice, members of the audience began screaming out curse words and phrases. Alice had to stop and wait till the cussing stopped and began her other comments about mining illnesses and suicides. At the mention of the word suicide, Zuma jumped up and screamed, "Stop the show!" ran up on the stage, and tackled Alice Bourne. Somehow, he managed to knock her down and grab the pistol she was holding in her hand. Some members of the audience began jumping up and moving towards the stage. Pat recognized the danger to Zuma, stood up, and fired his gun into the ceiling and everyone stopped. "Everyone get back into your seats and stay there. No one is going to leave this theatre. Move. *Now!*"

Zuma had told Pat that there would be officers posted outside and all Pat would have to do is press one of their alert numbers and they would enter the theatre and block all exits.

"I'm going to walk out with Ms. Bourne while the rest of you remain in your seats. If any of you try to prevent me from doing this, you will be arrested for interfering with an arrest. I am doing this to prevent a very bad accident from occurring and from harm coming to this most talented and creative person. Officers, give me a minute after I leave the theater with Ms. Bourne and then you may allow all the patrons to leave if they so desire. They, of course, are welcome to stay as the producer of the show might remain. I want all the officers here until the last patron leaves. No one is to touch anything on the stage."

In the car, Pat sat with Alice in the rear while Zuma drove.

"I realized what you were going to do when I heard you mention suicide, and I thought I heard you stress the word suicide and I had to stop you, Alice. I sensed what you were going to do. I know that would be your way of making your plays message more dramatic, but I just couldn't let you do that to yourself."

"I'm not grateful, Detective, though I appreciate your concern. I am going to jail and probably more than just a jail or prison sentence. I promised you I would give you information about the murders if I could finish the play. I fulfilled my promise to you as I have written everything that I wanted to tell you and it's in the mail right now."

"Do you want to speak now or shall I have to wait to get the mail?"

"Let's wait, Detective. This has been an emotional day, and I could actually use some quiet time in a solitary cell if you can do that for me, after you book me. If you think I'm a suicide risk, you should be able to get me a quiet cell where I can be observed. The letter should be arriving sometime in the next few days. I sent it snail mail. We can read it together in case you have any questions."

"I'll get you a quiet cell, Alice. It will be some distance from the other inmates. I need you to sign something indicating that we have told you your full rights and that you do not want to call your lawyer or make any phone calls."

"I'll sign. I don't want to call Irving, but I do want to call my producer. I assume I will be able to go home after one or two nights of rest here. You can put the ankle bracelet on and put a guard at my home when you're ready to release me. Now I'd like to call Christina."

The letter from Alice arrived at the precinct two days after Alice had been released. It was addressed to both Zuma and Vasquez.

I, Alice Munroe do admit that I shot and murdered Cynthia Goodling at Richard Slaters home. I hadn't intended to kill her, but I saw an opportunity to make it seem that she was the one who did it. It made sense to me since we both had the same feelings towards the SOB. I came to Slater's house with no intention of killing him. I wanted to, once again, plead my case for an opportunity to direct or for him to accept one of my scripts. When I came to his home, I noticed that the large French door was ajar. I looked in and I saw a woman sticking a gun in Slater's face. He was on his knees and she was standing over him. I knocked on the window and she turned around without changing the position of the gun. She must have recognized me for she waved for me to come in. I told her that I was sure that she had every right to be furious at Slater. I told her that I was also in rage at his treatment of me and of women. I asked her if she wanted to go through with it. She nodded her head yes and shot Slater twice. When she was done, she dropped the weapon. I picked it up and I shot her twice. I wiped off all the prints on the gun and left the scene. With this letter, I fulfill my promise to you, Detective Zuma, to provide you with information. I have no more information that I want to or am able to give you. Your search for suspects in the killing of Richard Slater and the women in his home is now over. I will await my trial.

"Boss, I guess she never intended to tell us anything else about the gang from West Virginia. She seems pretty cool about any trial, and it sounds like she has been moral about fulfilling her promise to you."

"And the trial will give her what the suicide would have given her: lots of publicity about mining issues in the country, and if the trial lasts a few days, she'll get more publicity than from the suicide that she was planning at the theatre. Let's pick her up. I'm sure that this time, she will make a call to her lawyer. Let's go together, Pat."

When Zuma and Pat arrived at the Bourne residence, there were about eight neighbors milling around in front.

"I've got a feeling, boss, that Big Alice is never going to trial."

Alice Bourne was dangling from a rope that had been tied around her neck. After cutting her down, Zuma and Pat found the suicide note.

> You were right, Detective Zuma. I was planning to do this in the theater. When you stopped me. But you know, Detective, we folks from West Virginia are a very determined lot. I'll never know what the impact of my play will be, but I know that I had to write it and feel at peace with what I am doing. Best wishes in your work. I do not wish you any success in pursing the deaths of those who were strike breakers.

"Pat, she was Big Alice in life and in death."

"She was, boss, but I can only think of her now as 'mountain mama.'"

CHAPTER 23

The funeral for Alice Bourne was attended by over one thousand people. The church was overflowing with speakers and TV screens in the streets for people to watch and hear the service. Christina Slater spoke about the lifelong struggle that Alice had in a world full of sexism and her fight to make it a level-playing field. She described her talents as a writer and a director and the loss that she will mean to all the people of the South, men and women who believe in justice. She also said she was starting a scholarship fund to award stipends that would support southern writers, women, and men who capture the genuine virtues of the South. The fund will be called the Alice Bourne Award for Creative Writing. Christina said she would start the fund by contributing a hundred thousand dollars. A band played "Country Roads" but this time no one sang. Many cried as the casket was removed from the church and made ready to be put on a plane and sent back to West Virginia. Zuma recognized that a few of the suspects were carrying the casket to the hearse. He knew they would not be allowed to get on a plane, but that there would be others, either from the service or back home, waiting to pay their respects to Alice Bourne. Many would feel obliged and privileged to thank and salute her for the service she had performed for them.

When Zuma and Pat were returning to the precinct, they got a call from Detective Malone.

"I didn't want to bother you during the service, but we got a call about another suicide. It's a male, and I'm in the apartment now. I cut down the body. The woman who called it in is waiting outside. I told her you would be here shortly.

"What's her relationship to the victim?"

"She said they had been living together for five years. Her name is Britanney Bell, and she says she knows you."

The name did not register with Zuma. He wondered if this could be connected to the other murders and how was it possible that it could be done at the same time that Bourne was being buried. Weren't all the suspects at the funeral? Are there more suspects unbeknownst to them?

"Ms. Bell, I know you told one of my men that you know me. Please forgive me if I don't recall how we met or know each other. I like to talk with you but first I want to see the body. Can you wait here? I'm going to ask Detective Vasquez to stay with you. I can put you in a car where its cooler and get you something to drink."

"I'll be fine, Detective. I will wait."

The detective escorted Zuma into the apartment. Zuma was struck with how colorful and artfully decorated the rooms were. There were lots of paintings on every wall of the apartment.

The body had a military uniform Zuma recognized was from the Israeli army. In addition, there was an emblem that indicated that the corpse had been a Seal.

The screw that had been inserted into the ceiling was a big one.

"This guy knew what he was doing. He had to get a big enough screw, strong rope, and had to calculate the length of the noose in relation to the height of the chair. His note left on his desk is simple."

Zuma picked up the note and read.

I'm sorry for what I have done. I hope you can
find it in your heart to forgive me. I could not
bear to live with myself any longer. All you wish
to know about me will be found in the box
under this note. The money is for you to do with
whatever you wish.

Zuma opened the box. There were fifty $1,000 bills on top. Zuma knew that these were rare and someone had to go to a lot of trouble to amass them. Under the money, there were a bunch of letters including love letters. Zuma counted the names of seven different women. One of them, reminded him of his wedding vows and wanted her wedding ring back. Another two were from children who said they wanted nothing to do with him. There was also an award for his having participated in the successful raid at Entebbe. This was an incredible air strike, flying in the dead of night and evading Egyptian intelligence, landing in the dark in Uganda and rescuing 102 Israelis citizens who were being watched by their captors and held in Uganda by Adi Amin.

"This guy was quite the guy. He was a war hero, married with lovers galore, and living here with another woman. I wonder what he meant by not being able to live with himself. Is that guilt, Detective Zuma?"

"I don't know, Malone. We need to speak to the woman. I wonder how he made enough money to run around. Maybe not everything there is to know was contained in this draw. Maybe this has nothing to do with our other ongoing investigations, but as you may know Malone, I'm not a believer in coincidences. Let's go speak with our lady in waiting."

Britanney Bell was distraught. Pat Vasquez was offering her Kleenex as she cried, but in between tears, she talked about how she had gone to the theater with friends and he had seemed in a good mood. He said that he was going to spend the afternoon painting and hoped that by the time she came home that he would have finished the painting of the desert scene he was working on. When she calmed down, she looked at Zuma.

"I met you because my ex-boyfriend had treated your wife. He was an oncologist and she must have been very grateful because there was an evening when you and your wife and Murray and I were in the same restaurant. She came over with you and said hello and was effusive in her appreciation. We were introduced but it was very brief. I hope she is still doing well."

"She got over the cancer but, unfortunately, she was killed in an auto accident by a hit and run. That was about six or seven years ago."

"I'm sorry to hear that. I think we met about ten years ago.

"Ms. Bell…"

"Please call me Britanney."

"Britanney, I was struck with the color and the number of paintings you had."

"I'm an interior decorator and Benyaminy had a hobby while he was in the military and when he left, he took up painting full time."

She began repeating he story of how he was planning to finish the painting while she was away at the theater. Zuma just let her finish.

"I would like to ask you more questions but understand that this might not be the best time. Would you like to set an appointment for tomorrow?"

"I can talk now, but I need to call my children and a few of my very close friends. I'm sure they will want to come over and spend time with me. Can you wait?"

"Of course."

During the four phone calls which took about two hours, Zuma and Pat went through the letters and wrote down any information they could possibly use: addresses, phone numbers, and dates. The phone which had been lying on top of the box of letter revealed that the last call matched the letter from his wife in Colorado.

"Pat, I don't think we can just call her to tell her the news. You need to hop on a plane tonight and speak to Janet Laslett. I'll personally call these others when I get back to the office. Let's finish up here. You might pick something up which would help you when you talk with the wife. Alert her that you are making a routine investigation, but you need to make an appointment with her."

"Boss, you don't think this suicide is related to the other murders? I take that back. I know you and with that toothpick already out, I know you are thinking of how they might be related."

"Yes, Pat. I'm thinking. This man was deeply devious and a well-trained killer. Maybe he hired himself out? Maybe the WV gang used him for their dirty work? Maybe it is a coincidence. But we are going to have to work on discovering if there are any connections. If nothing shows up, I will judge this as just a coincidence. He lived a well-heeled lifestyle, and he couldn't make it off his painting and his pension. Get going and interview the wife in Colorado."

The ad had been successful. He ran it in a magazine devoted to the newest in guns which he knew would be read by gun owners and those needing help to track people down.

> Trained in discovering missing or lost persons,
> uncovering false identities; excellent marksman;
> no questions asked; military background; cash only.
> Send request to PO Box 102, Denver, Colorado.

A response came within a few weeks.

> Please call me at the following number: 310-458-7777. I will destroy the phone after we speak. I am hoping you can meet me in Los Angeles. When we talk, I will propose a project. You can tell me how much cash you will want for the work. I will give you half up front and the other half when the assignment is complete. I am prepared to bring and pay $25,000 to our first meeting. If this is acceptable, tell me when you will be able to meet. I can do it anytime day or night. There is an Apple store in the Century City Mall. I would like to meet you in a public space. Tell me what you will be wearing, and I will find you.

He was surprised to see that it was a woman who approached him and she established that she was the one who had corresponded with PO Box 102. She had written the name of the person on a small piece of paper and asked him to memorize it. When he indicated he had, she said, "I want him killed." Here is $25,000. When you complete this, I will send you another $25,000 in cash. I will FedEx it to the post office box. He wanted to know where he could find her if the second payment was never received. She was stumped. She wanted no more contact than this one. He refused to proceed unless there was a way, he could contact her in case the money was not sent. If she wanted this execution she would have to play by his rules.

She agreed to give him all the money in advance but needed to go to the bank. He agreed to come back tomorrow but asked that they meet in a different location at 3:00 p.m. She didn't like playing by a man's rules but realized that she had no choice. If he was successful, she would feel enormous relief.

CHAPTER 24

"Boss, Jane Laslett was straightforward and seemed honest but not much help. The guy sent monthly payments to her and his kids. He visited her about once a month. Never told her how he got money or where he lived when he wasn't here. He did not have much to do with the kids. She didn't like it but felt he was reliable when it came to cash. She assumed he was with other women. He was restless and would never be able to make a commitment. She believed it was part of what happened to him during the war. He had seen too many deaths."

"This is a puzzler, Pat. He had seen too many deaths but may have been involved in more killings? I don't know what to make of that."

"Boss, you always say, it's sex, money, power, or drugs. This guy may be pursuing three out of four."

Zuma was stumped. How did he earn money to keep up the lifestyle he had and support ex-wives and children? Where could fifty grand in these rare $1000 bills have come from? And if this war hero was connected to the WV gang, how did he make that connection and what was he doing with or for them?

"Let's start with those bills. Call the Fed and see if they have any record of a request for a large number of bills. We can give them the numbers. They might lead us to a bank where they came from. If we get that, we will know who withdrew the money. We need to check every phone number and see if they are connected to any of the people we know are from WV. Get Malone to cross-check the number in the phone with the ones we have. Pat, you call the Feds and follow up the money stuff."

"Detective Zuma, the phone numbers that were similar belong to Christina Marshall and her father."

"Boss, the Feds say it was a bank in Santa Monica, First Republic, that made the request. When I called them, they said I had to come down to verify who I was."

"Good work to both of you. Pat, lets head over to the bank together. You drive."

Once Zuma and Pat revealed their identities to the manager, he pulled up the deposit record. Christina Marshall had been making deposits of $4,000 every week for the past year. Zuma knew that anything under $5,000 never had to be reported to the Federal government.

"Did she bring in the money herself?"

"No, most of the times she came with an older man. She spoke very little."

Zuma noticed that after every deposit, a withdrawal in the amount of $3,000 had been made.

"Were these withdrawals in large denominations?"

"No, she only requested $100 bills. The clerks had a name for her. They called her 'the hundred dollar silent one.'"

"Our little actress needed cash for the play but not this much. A weekly deposit means that a routine had been established. And you and I know, Pat, drug dealers have regular routines."

"We could probably pick them up pretty quickly, boss."

"I know Pat. But they are not going to tell us where they got the money from."

Christina had not heard from the man she hired for a week and believed she had been played. When she read about a suicide in

Santa Monica that had been committed by an Israeli hero, she knew she had lost the fifty grand. She believed that Zuma was the only one smart enough to figure out what she and her father had been doing, and she wanted him out of the way so that the goals that she and her father had set could be achieved.

Zuma knew that the only way he could establish that Christina had been involved in the murders were to see where she was getting the money from. Was she picking it up? Was it being delivered to her and by whom?

The tail on Mr. Marshall led Zuma and Pat to the LAX Airport. While he was sipping his coffee, two young men approached him, sat down, and passed him a small briefcase. They chatted for a while, and then both of the younger men got up headed to the departing planes sign while Mr. Marshall headed towards the exit.

"Pat, go after those two guys. No guns unless absolutely necessary. Tell them they are under arrest for drug trafficking. I'll take care of Marshall."

Zuma stopped him as he was about to exit the airport.

"You're under arrest, Mr. Marshall for drug dealing."

Marshall laughed as they started to read him his rights. "I have no drugs and I want to call my lawyer. I don't have to show you what's in this briefcase unless you have a warrant."

The three men were taken to the precinct and Irving Silverberg, Marshalls lawyer, was waiting for them.

"What are the charges, Detective Zuma? You need a warrant. My clients do not have to answer any questions unless there is a specific charge."

"Irving, let me tell the detective a few things."

"I advise you against that."

"Detective, we have money in this briefcase. It is money I was planning to put into a bank. I will then withdraw some of it and send it back to West Virginia. We have set up a fund for all the families of the strikers. Their children will be the main beneficiaries, since we are setting up college funds. We are also building homes for the strikers and providing them with health insurance. We are replanting the mountains with local plants, shrubs, and trees. We even gave money to the goddamn mine owners to put on air filters over their exhausts so our citizens would not be poisoned. This was the plan that Christiana and I devised."

"That's wonderful, Mr. Marshall. But where is the money coming from?"

"Detective, I told you I would only tell you a few things."

Zuma knew he had no charges against the two men or Marshall.

"Could the two of you tell me how you know Mr. Marshall?"

"Detective. I told you before that we are a tight-knit family. I think you would have guessed by now."

"Hi, Detective. I'm Kurt and this is Mike. We're both Marshalls. We're his sons."

CHAPTER 25

"What do you think of the plan?"

"As long as the drugs don't end up anywhere in the South, I can go for it."

"I can guarantee that, Dad. I want to explain how we can guarantee the drugs will be heading north and our plan to earn money for our foundation."

"Let me hear the plan."

"Fresh fruit is delivered every week to Charleston by truck. We meet the truck and before they deliver it to local stores, we make our purchases of bananas, pears, and oranges. We take the fruit and put our quarter sized vials inside the unripe fruit. This is the only real labor on our part besides driving. We wait for it to ripen so the cuts won't be easily seen. We load the fruit in our two cars and make sure that some of the fruit has not been injected just in case we get stopped. We can offer fruit to any police officers or any other people who think we're suspicious and want to inspect what we are carrying. We are carrying drugs that have a street value of over a thousand dollars. Our cover story is we are delivering this to our poor relatives in the neighboring cites of Charleston. The drive is never more than three hours, and we can make it back in the same day.

Since we are white, our stories of helping poor relatives will be believed. Our cars are shabby looking and we will dress with old, worn clothes There are four cities within a three-hour drive of Charleston. There is Columbus and Cincinnati in Ohio, Pittsburgh in Pennsylvania, and Lexington, Kentucky. Two cites can be done in a one day roundtrip. These are the gateway cities for the drugs travelling to the north. That's what I meant when I could guarantee that they would not be sold to our southern brethren. We each do two cities a week, taking turns to not do the same city in one week. In that way, even if the police stop us and become familiar with us, they will believe we are doing our weekly delivery of food to our relatives. We go out of our way to find out what fruit they prefer and tell them we will be sure to have it ready for them on our next weekly trip. When we deliver the drugs to the addresses I have, we get paid in cash. I think we should be making $500 from a drop in a city. We each make a grand a trip, and that's four grand a week. We send most of the cash to you and keep a little for our expenses. You put it in in the bank that has our foundation account. All the Marshalls have worked hard to establish for our community, the foundation with the name we love and are proud of."

"What is the name you have come up with? I can't figure out what it could possibly stand for. What does SHINE Foundation stand for?"

"Dad, we though you would guess. Its one of the proudest things we have in our culture. You taught it to us, growing up. Even during the strike, you said it was important for us to maintain."

"I give up. Tell me already."

"Southern Hospitality in Everything."

"You have my blessings. I look forward to seeing a rebuilt town with sidewalks that aren't flooded by rains, mountains that have shrubs and trees, and being able to go outside look at the rebuilt homes and breathing fresh air. Mostly, I look forward to seeing West Virginia people smiling as they walk down their streets and greet each other with the sound of hope in their voice."

"Dad, maybe this would be a good time and better and easier on all of us if we were to tell Zuma what we did to raise money."

"Let me talk with Silverberg, Detective. I would only need a couple of minutes to confer with our lawyer."

"No problem."

"Detective Zuma, I want it to be noted for the record that Mr. Marshall's two sons are being cooperative and volunteering information regarding their selling and transporting of drugs."

"I will note that for the record."

The boys proceeded to reveal the details of their illegal efforts. When Zuma asked for the names and addresses in the cities they traveled to they balked, and said it would probably mean that would cost them their lives. Silverberg told Zuma that he could put ankle bracelets on the two and that they would be ready to plead guilty when the time came for their trial."

It was Zuma's time to ask for a few moments to talk with Pat in private.

"What have we got, Pat? Not much more than before. We still have unsolved murders, no understanding of what our war hero was doing with all that cash, where Christina fits into this, and what Mr. Marshall's connections to any of this except his approval of the fund raising for the foundation."

"Mr. Marshall, since your boys have helped us with important details, is there any information that you would like to provide to us.?"

"Detective, are you trying to take advantage of my southern hospitality?"

Zuma laughed. "No, just of your good sense and smarts."

"If you can guarantee that my sons and I go to the same prison, I would be willing to give you some information."

"Dad. Please don't do this. It's not necessary. We can do the time just fine."

"I know that. It would be nice if when we get out, the Marshall family can all be together again. Our prison records will be behind us, the misery of the strike, and what it has caused will be dimmer and we can take great pride for what we did and have done for our town of Mongahlia."

"I don't know if I can guarantee that I can recommend to the court that the three of you be assigned to the same prison, but a strong recommendation is all I can do."

Zuma waited. Pat and he looked directly into the Marshalls' eyes. Mr. Marshall paused, looked at his sons and nodded his head indicating that he was going to talk. They nodded back indicating their agreement.

"I'm responsible for the murders of the strikers."

CHAPTER 26

When Christina Marshall heard the news about her father's confessions, she was furious. She screamed at Silverberg, calling him all kinds of names including anti-Semitic slurs. He did not respond, laughing to himself about her father's complete failure to teach his daughter southern hospitality. After a while, when he sensed that he could get a word in, he suggested that this was not only what her father wanted for himself but for his family and that his vision after serving time in prison and getting a reduced sentence for confessing and for pleading guilty was of a united family back in their rejuvenated town in West Virginia. She saw the wisdom in her father's confession for the family but was still worried about Zuma. He might not believe the confessions, and she cursed at the failure of her hired gun to succeed in getting rid of Zuma. And she was right, Zuma and Pat went over every murder that each striker had suffered. They soon realized that it would have been impossible for Mr. Marshall to have done some of them since he had been under surveillance at the time some of the murders had been committed.

"Pat, I see only once conclusion staring us in the face."

"Me too, boss. It's the actress and star of the show, Christina."

"Pat, we've got to put all of this this together. We're sure it was Alice Bourne who killed Cynthia Goodling, the aspiring director. We have her confession, a body, and her motives were clear. We're pretty sure that it was Christina who killed Saul Slater. Her motive was also clear. More money for her and the family. That's two deaths. Officers Sanchez and Knox were shot, and we think it was the WV gang but don't know who, although Marshall confessed to those murders. The motive there is revenge with the same motive being involved in the gang murders of the men who broke the strike. These include Haskin and Roman. That's four deaths."

"Detective, Christina Slater is wanting to see you. She says its urgent."

Christina was forceful as she spoke. "Detective Zuma, I won't beat around the bush. My father did not do all those murders. It was impossible for him to do them all and I can prove to you that he did not do all of them."

"And your here to tell us what? To tell us who did them?"

"That is exactly why I'm here. I did them."

It took about half an hour before Silverberg arrived at the precinct, and after trying to convince her not to do so, he helped Christina compose her confession. He did this out of hearing from Zuma. Christina confessed to killing Saul Slater and Haskin and Roman. Zuma booked her and a hearing was set for bail. Because the judge allowed Christina out on bail, she was making the most of the news and TV coverage. She talked to reporters about her guilt over the crimes and not wanting her father to cover up for her. She said people would understand her desire for revenge if they went to see the play she was producing.

Next morning's paper had lead stories of the confession, how the crimes were solved, and some about the victims. Zuma read the headlines to Claudia.

"Young Starlet Confesses to murders of Revenge. String of Murders Solved by Chief of City Police and Local Detective."

It was this last headline that caught Zuma by surprise, and when he turned on the TV there was Thompson extolling the cooperation between the cities of Los Angeles and Santa Monica.

"My God, what is he running for? He's already head of the biggest police force in the country. He must have his eye on something bigger. Maybe he's aiming for political office? Maybe in government? Homeland security? The man is more ambitious than I realized."

"Your view of him seems to have changed quite a bit, darling. Do you think you will be able to work with him in the future?"

"I don't know. It will depend on the case, but I will be more cautious. I need to figure out how to get Pat on the tube so he can get some credit and move the attention away from Thompson.

During dinner while Pat, Zuma, and Claudia were celebrating the victory, Pat casually mentioned that Britanny Bell had invited him to go to that Friday night thing that Jews have. He wondered out loud if he was doing the right thing

Claudia jumped in. "It's called Shabbat. You pronounce the first syllable as if you telling someone to be quiet 'Shhhh' and the second syllable is pronounced as you would say bottom. The accent is on the first syllable. What is your problem?"

"She had been a suspect, she is older, she is white, and a bit more religious than I am and, of course, it's a different religion."

"The case is solved, so she is no longer a suspect. All the other stuff you mentioned is just an excuse. We never know who we can fall in love with. Pat, most of the songs I hum and have introduced you to involve actual places, like Cape Cod, Ventura Highway, Country Roads. Others are often named after women like Laura, Roxanne, or Elanor Rigby. But some songs are more philosophical. One of the best pieces of advice about life and relationships is sung by Mick Jagger of the Rolling Stones."

"Don't know him or the group, boss."

The wisdom is in the title of the song. I suggest you listen and listen carefully to the words 'You Can't Always Get What You Want."

"I know that, boss. Nothing new there for me."

"Yeah, but the next line would be new for you when he sings, 'But If You Try Sometime, You'll Get What You Need.'"

"Pat, I as a woman, stand behind that. We can discover what we need after we give up aiming for the sky and realizing we need less."

You don't need a Latina, a Catholic, or a younger woman. By focusing on what you don't have, you don't allow yourself to see that you might have, indeed do have, what you need. So, go try."

Zuma was agreeing with Claudia and encouraging Pat when a call came in to Zuma.

"Pat, Claudia, there has been another murder. So much for the case being solved. Lets meet with Thompson."

Christina Marshall was dead. The shooter had put two bullets into her heart from close range. The body had been propped on a bench in Santa Monica on the bluffs. An early morning jogger had spotted it and called it in. Zuma was shocked and stumped.

"Pat, no one from the WV gang would have done this. The play was successful and going strong so the actors were working and possibilities of anger or jealousy would not be operating. Who knew Christina Marshall outside the close-knit WV gang, the strikers and those who refused to strike?"

"Boss, I think that the guys who refused to strike would be most likely. Only three were left of the seven. All of them would have motives for revenge and retaliation. Should I bring them in?"

"They had plenty of time to get back at the WV gang. Why just now? Let's wait till we do a thorough search of the crime scene. Maybe the bullets are traceable. Let's put a rush on the trace. If revenge is a motive, there will be others who can be murdered."

"Boss, good news about the bullet tracing. They were traced to a weapon being held in Chief Thompson's station."

"Well that narrows it down to who? As I said, it's not the WV gang. Why would any other office in Thompson's precinct want to kill her? Let's see what we can find out about the gun."

"Boss, the gun had not been signed out in over a month. The last time was for practice on the firing range. There were no fingerprints but traces of powder revealed the weapon had been fired in the last twenty-four to forty-eight hours. Camera footage showed an officer checking out the weapon last month and returning it after an hour. There was no footage of anyone checking out the gun since that time.

"Chief Thompson, how is it possible that this gun came out and there is no signing for it and no footage?"

"Zuma, if I had footage and a signature, the SOB would be in lockup by now."

"I would like to examine all the footage in the past forty-eight hours. I imagine I will find some erasures after the last month's checkout. Would you like to do this with me or should I do this with Pat?"

"You can do this with Vaszuez. Im going to try and figure this out. I will go over the files again and check for anyone not only from West Virgina but from the South. It had to be someone who knew her from earlier or from now."

CHAPTER 27

It took Zuma and Pat about four hours to go through the tape. They found a tape erasure of two hours shortly before the murder of Cynthia Marshall. This wasn't enough direct evidence to get anyone convicted. It now became a questdion of who had access to the tapes. Was there more than one person? For the first time, Zuma thought that if it was Thompson and he was arrested and found innocent in a trial, Thompson's political ambitions and his policing career would be destroyed. He did not want to do anything to a colleague who had served so long. But who else could it be?"

The TV news made Zuma drop his coffee cup and it spilled onto Claudia's side of their breakfast nook.

"The Chief of Police in Los Angeles, Chief Robert Thompson died last night or early this morning in an apparent suicide. His body was found by his wife in the chief's study at their home in midcity. There was a note, but its contents are not being revealed. Officers are at the scene and talking to Mrs. Thompson. She indicated that she would be making a statement as soon as the officers have finished talking with her. We will have more news as events develop."

"Sorry for the coffee spill, honey. I am shocked and very surprised. He did not seem like the kind of man who would off himself. Remember, I said he had a big ego."

"Maybe he was ill and had a terminal illness."

"Could be, but I don't think so. I can't tell you more now, but he was under suspicion for possible murder. I'm leaving right now and picking up Pat. I need to see the note."

On the way to Thompsons' home, the two detectives heard the wife's statement.

"I know all Los Angelinos will grieve with me at the loss of this man and his wonderful leadership. It is loss for our city and its citizens as well as to me personally. Please allow me to have some privacy in these next few days. There will be an announcement if a day or so about funeral arrangements."

"Boss, what did the note say?"

"Pat, it definitely was a suicide. He knew how to do it without screwing it up. I greatly underestimated this man's ability to deceive and plot and overestimated his devotion to his police force and the city."

"Did his note talk about his plotting and deceiving? Tell me more, boss."

"There were two notes, Pat, one to the wife and the other to you and me.

"That is strange, boss. A note to the two of us."

"The note to the wife indicated her benefits what she has to do to put the house in her name, and $10,000 that he will be giving to to the city for increasing the diversity training of officers. He said that the money should be used to hire you and I to do the training. He asked his wife to hand the note to me and asked her not to open it. He also expressed his deep regrets and sorry to his wife about his duplicity.

"What about the note to us, boss?"

"Heres the note, Pat. Mrs. Thompson said it was ours to keep. I don't think she read it."

> Dear Detectives Zuma and Vasquez:
> I want you to know all the details of my involvment
> in the murders of the past few months. I regret
> that I could not be as honest a detective as the
> two of you are. I admire your integriy and your
> committmenet to justice. Once I realized that
> there was a WV gang in my precinct and who they
> were, I saw an opportunity to make money. I was
> planning to use the money for a political career. I

would not go after them in exchange for money. I made this agreement with Christina and her dad. He covered for them. I guess he did not care about their revenge motives. In retrospect neither did I. Marshall received money every week from Christina. Do you recall how you wondered that she seemed to be she withdrawing a lot more than necessary? I realized that. When Christina and her dad were going to jail, I knew the money payments would stop. But now, I realized that they had been making a lot more money than ever revealed to me.

"Geez, Louise. Boss, the guy was really an operator. I think you're going to tell me that he was going to go after more money, but how?"

"He was an operator, Pat, and here's how he did it."

I found out the address in Charleston where drugs were being delivered and saw thats how I coul make a lot more money. I would sell in the South. It would not be a problem for me to get ex-cons. I could threaten them with parole violation if they would not work for me. The folks who delivered drugs welcomed me as someone who was going to spread sales over a larger area. When Marshall found out that I was selling in the South and he got furious, at that point I knew he was going to blow the whistle on me. I had nothing on them, and they had nothing to lose. They were pleased that the foundation had done what it was designed to do. Nothing more needed to be done. I knew I was done for.

"What about the other murders, boss? Not all of them are accounted for. Did he say anydthing about that?"

"He did, Pat."

> I killed the innocent bystander from the DMV. I did that dto throw your investigation into turmoil. I also shot my own two men, Sanchez and Knox, but was glad they survived. You can tell them that I shot them. Because I had access to the security tapes, I could erases the times when I used the unmarked cars in the department. I could use them at will.

"Boss, this man was not only smart he was diabolical."
"Pat, he had the makings of a politician."
"The poor guy was in the wrong line of work."
"Pat, let's be grateful we are in the right line of work. Let's be greatful that we have integrity and are not greedy. I think we should all celebrate. Let's go to the Shangri-La. Dinner is on me."
"I can't do that tonight, boss. I have been invited by Britanney Bell for the Friday night stuff. I still haven't figured out how to pronounce it correctly, so I just call it 'shop us.'"

—∞—

"Joe what's your prediction about Pat and the Bell lady? Do you think it's going to be more than a fling?"
"Claudia I thought you would have more insight into that than me. I know Pat. He wants a relationship, a family, and children. I'm not sure that is what she wants. But I think you know women better than I do. In fact, I'm sure you do."
"Joe, if Pat falls for her, she will be able to convince him that she is all he needs. She may not even have to convince him. He may discover on his own that he is getting what he needs."
"I guess he'll be just like me. You, my darling Claudia, are all that I need."

THE END

www.ingramcontent.com/pod-product-compliance
Lightning Source LLC
Chambersburg PA
CBHW032035180726
48284CB00008B/2604